St. Charles Public Library
St. Charles, IL 60174

W9-BZA-324

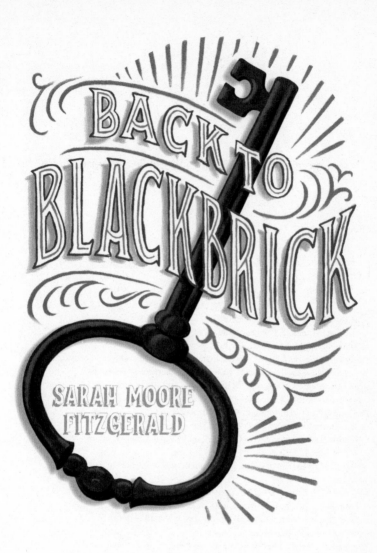

BACK TO BLACKBRICK

SARAH MOORE FITZGERALD

MARGARET K. McELDERRY BOOKS

New York London Toronto Sydney New Delhi

In memory of Paul Stanley Moore: Dad extraordinaire.

MARGARET K. McELDERRY BOOKS
An imprint of Simon & Schuster Children's Publishing Division
1230 Avenue of the Americas, New York, New York 10020
This book is a work of fiction. Any references to historical events, real people,
or real places are used fictitiously. Other names, characters, places, and
events are products of the author's imagination, and any resemblance to
actual events or places or persons, living or dead, is entirely coincidental.
Text copyright © 2013 by Sarah Moore Fitzgerald
Jacket illustrations copyright © 2013 by James Tierney
Previously published in 2013 in Great Britain by Orion Children's Books
First U.S. edition 2013
All rights reserved, including the right of reproduction in whole or in part in
any form.
MARGARET K. McELDERRY BOOKS is a trademark of Simon & Schuster, Inc.
For information about special discounts for bulk purchases, please
contact Simon & Schuster Special Sales at 1-866-506-1949 or
business@simonandschuster.com.
The Simon & Schuster Speakers Bureau can bring authors to your live
event. For more information or to book an event, contact the Simon
& Schuster Speakers Bureau at 1-866-248-3049 or visit our website at
www.simonspeakers.com.
Book design by Debra Sfetsios-Conover
The text for this book is set in ITC Caslon STD.
Manufactured in the United States of America
10 9 8 7 6 5 4 3 2 1
0813 FFG
CIP data is available from the Library of Congress.
ISBN 978-1-4424-8155-8 (hardcover)
ISBN 978-1-4424-8157-2 (eBook)

Of this at least I feel assured, that there is no such thing as forgetting possible to the mind; a thousand accidents may and will interpose a veil between our present consciousness and the secret inscriptions on the mind; accidents of the same sort will also rend away this veil; but alike, whether veiled or unveiled, the inscription remains for ever, just as the stars seem to withdraw before the common light of day, whereas in fact we all know that it is the light which is drawn over them as a veil, and that they are waiting to be revealed when the obscuring daylight shall have withdrawn.

Thomas De Quincey
Confessions of an English Opium-Eater

Chapter 1

MY GRANDDAD was pretty much the cleverest person I ever met, so it was strange in the end to see the way people treated him—as if he was a complete moron. We were waiting for a train one day, not bothering anyone, when this boy said to me, "Hey. Hey you. What's wrong with the old man?"

In fairness, my granddad did happen to be in the middle of quite a long conversation with a lamppost. But still, it didn't give the boy the right to be so nosy.

I walked a bit closer to the boy, and I whispered:

"He suffers from a rare condition that makes him randomly violent to anyone who asks stupid questions about people they've never met."

That very same week me and Granddad saw this program all about how Albert Einstein was always looking for his keys and wearing odd shoes and not brushing his hair for weeks on end.

"See, Granddad?" I said to him. "Einstein was exactly the same as you are. And no one ever thought there was anything wrong with *his* brain."

3 0053
01060
1840

"No one except for his teachers, who apparently thought he was an imbecile," my granddad replied.

The next day he asked me where the toilet was. And the day after that he looked at me suddenly and he said, "Maggie, Maggie, what's the plan of action now? When are we all going home?" which was kind of confusing, seeing as there was no plan of action, and seeing as we already *were* at home. And also seeing as my name is not Maggie.

My name is Cosmo. When I'm a legal adult, I'm going to change it by deed poll. I've checked it out, and it's fairly straightforward.

The first time Granddad peed in the dishwasher was when me and my gran realized we were going to have to make a few changes. For one thing, we got into the habit of putting the superhot cycle on twice.

He began to repeat things over and over, and I knew that there was definitely something wrong, because he hadn't usually been a repetitive sort of guy. It got to be pretty annoying. He began to forget the kinds of things that you'd never imagine anyone could forget, like for example that my brother, Brian, was dead, even though by then he'd been dead for quite a while. Granddad got this idea that Brian was actually in the kitchen, completely alive, and ready to make cups of tea for anyone who shouted at him.

"BRIAN! BRIAN!" he'd yell. "DO US A FAVOR LIKE A GOOD FELLOW, AND BRING US A CUP OF TEA!"

So then *I'd* usually have to go off and make the stupid tea. Granddad always said, "Ah, fantastic," right after he took the first sip, as if drinking a cup of tea was the best thing ever.

When he started to get up in the middle of the night and wander around the house, poking about and searching in drawers and stuff, me and my gran kept having to follow him. We'd have to think of quite clever ways to convince him to go back to bed, which usually took ages. He'd sometimes have gone out into the garden before we'd even woken up, and we'd run out to him where he stood shivering, thin and empty. Like a shadow.

I'd say, "Granddad, what are you doing out here in the dark like this?" And he'd say, "I don't know really. I used to love the dark."

And after that my gran would sit with him as if he was the one who needed to be comforted, even though it was me who'd been woken up in the middle of the night. He would say, "Oh, my girl," in a way that made it sound like Granny Deedee was someone quite young, which obviously she isn't. And she'd look down at his hands and stroke them and she'd tell him how beautiful they were.

Don't get me wrong—I mean, you could say a lot of nice things about my granddad, because he was a great guy and everything—but I really don't think you could say his hands were beautiful. For one thing, they were old and brown and bent like the roots of a tree. And for another thing, instead of an index finger he had a kind of stump on his right hand that only went as far as his first knuckle. It wasn't that noticeable except when he was trying to point at something.

Whenever I asked him what happened to that finger, he would look down and his eyes would go all round and he would say, "Good God! My finger. It's missing! Assemble a search party!"

It was kind of a joke that me and him had before he got sick. Nobody else got it.

I tried to talk to my gran about Granddad's memory, but she pretended it really wasn't that big a deal. She said we would do our best for him for as long as we could, but eventually we'd have to tell Uncle Ted, who at the time was living in San Francisco being a scientist and never answering his phone.

"Aren't there brain pills or something that Granddad can take?"

"Cosmo, love, he's already on lots of medication."

"Well, no offense, Gran, but you'd better go back to the doctor with him and change the dose."

"It's not the dose," she said. "It's the illness."

I didn't think that was a very constructive attitude. I told her I knew for a fact that there were loads of doctors who didn't have that much of a clue what they were even talking about. I started telling her about this one guy I'd seen on the True Stories channel who'd had a heart attack because they'd given him rat poison instead of cholesterol pills, but all Gran said was, "Oh, for goodness' sake, Cosmo, will you please stop it?" which was quite cranky of her if you ask me. She never used to be grumpy like that, no matter how many things I told her about.

Later that night I googled "memory loss," and I honestly didn't know why I hadn't done it sooner. It turns out there's a load of information for people in our situation. The very first link I clicked on was a website called:

THE MEMORY CURE
Proven strategies to delay and reverse age-related memory loss when someone you love starts to forget.

Those glittery words of hope shone from the screen, making me blink, and I could feel pints of relief pouring through my body, right down into my toes.

Chapter 2

THE MEMORY CURE website had excellent advice written out in handy actions and clear language that anyone could understand:

ACTION NUMBER 1: Talk to your loved one about times gone by. Use old photos of family and friends to initiate conversations about the past. You'll be surprised the things that such conversations will awaken.

In the corner of the living room there were photographs of all of us—pictures of my mum and my uncle Ted when they were young, and there was one of Granddad Kevin and Granny Deedee when they were not that young, but not that old, either, both of them looking into the distance in the same direction. There were also quite humiliating shots of me when I was a naked baby, with my brother, Brian.

I wouldn't have minded being named Brian. But it was my brother who got the nonpathetic name, not me. I said to my gran that I thought it wasn't fair, especially now that he didn't need his name anymore because he was dead. She said, "Darling, I know you don't mean that about your lovely brother, whose name will always belong to him," and I said, "No, no, of course I don't," even though I actually did.

"Granddad, who's this?" I said to him, pointing at one of my baby pictures.

"I don't seem to be able to recall," he said.

"Do you know who I am *now*?" I said, prodding my chest.

"No," he said. "I'm really very sorry."

I told him not to worry, that it was okay, even though obviously there's nothing okay about forgetting your own grandson.

People go through phases, and a lot of them come out the other side perfectly fine. I don't think you should write someone off just because they occasionally get a bit mixed-up and have to be shown where the toilet is.

At dinner that night Granddad frowned and chewed his food very slowly, not saying anything for ages. Then he looked up at my gran and he said, "Where's Brian?"

"Oh dear, now, don't distress yourself," my gran said to him, which was kind of condescending as far as I was concerned.

"Brian fell out of a window," I said helpfully.

"Did he?" said my granddad.

"Yes, my dear," my gran said, moving closer to him and softly patting him on the hand, "I'm afraid he did."

"He's dead now, isn't that right?" he said.

"Yes, he is," my gran replied.

"Oh," my granddad said. He clenched his jaw, and he kept brushing something invisible off his sweater. "Yes, that's what I thought. I mean, of course. I knew that." And he put his hand flat on his forehead and let out this shuddery sigh, and we all stayed quiet for a while, listening to the ticking of the clock on the wall.

There was nothing on the Memory Cure website that showed you what to do if talking about the past made the person you love start to cry, so me and my gran tried to move quickly on to cheering him up by talking about other people that Granddad loved, which was a bit difficult, seeing as many of them had disappeared off to San Francisco or Australia.

ACTION NUMBER 2:

Label common household items and images clearly.
As long as your loved one's reading capacity remains, this is a good way to help out with their day-to-day functioning.

I set up this quite good system by writing instructions on Post-its and sticking them all over the place. They said things like: "Open the fridge and take out the CHEESE," "This is the TOILET, which is for PEEING into," and "This is the DISHWASHER (for washing DISHES)."

I also wrote out people's names and stuck them on all the photos:

"Brian (your grandson—DEAD)"

"Uncle Ted (your son—in San Francisco)"

"Sophie (your daughter—drumming up business in Sydney)"

On my gran's picture I wrote, "Deedee (your wife)."

Those signs worked pretty well, except for Brian's, which didn't have that great an effect on any of us. I had to take it down quite quickly. It's one thing knowing that you've got a dead brother. It's another thing having to read it every single time you sit down to eat a bowl of cereal.

So I wrote a new sign that said: "Brian (your grandson—gone away for a while)."

That seemed to comfort Granddad, and in a funny kind of way it comforted me, too. If you read something often enough, part of you can start to believe it. Even if it is a lie and even if you've written the lie yourself.

My gran said I worried about the strangest things, like the house falling down. Everyone said it was because my brother had died. They thought that me worrying all the time was my way of being sad. I disagreed. Tragedy isn't the thing that makes the world a stressful place; it's the *chance* of tragedy that makes it stressful, and I guess that's what tormented me. Constantly being frightened about losing the things that I needed most—it was exhausting.

But it was never so bad when I was with my granddad. Whenever I started to get freaked out about something or other, he always used to notice. He would spot this little bead of worry rising from somewhere deep inside me before I'd even noticed it myself. And whenever he saw that, he would come over a bit closer to me and then he would say, "Cosmo, my old pal, I think it's time for a bit of rest, don't you?" And he might suggest that perhaps I'd like to have a bath. And sooner or later I would say, "Yes, I think I would." And then I would have a bath and he would light this big ancient old candle and put it on the shelf.

He'd have lit a fire by the time I came out of the bathroom, and I'd feel all clean and warm. Granddad liked to read stories to me from old books with hard dark covers by people like Charles Dickens. The stories usually had children in them who were stuck in orphanages or who were sick and poor but very cheerful all the same. They were about people who were forced to work in terrible conditions but loved each other and were polite and did not complain and were very loyal to their family members no matter what.

I would listen to his croaky old voice and I'd feel pretty cozy, and I would have been led away from whatever it was that was making me feel panicky, and instead I would feel soothed and cared for. I'd look at his old face, and the shadows would flicker and flash all around us because the fire would be big and lively by then. I'd feel calmer and more okay. I'd go to bed, and by the next day I'd be more or less fine again.

There was clattering and banging in the kitchen. I came down to see what all the noise was about, ready for the next emergency. But Granddad was making a cheese sandwich for breakfast. He grinned at me. I was delighted. My memory cure tactics were obviously beginning to kick in, and he was suddenly making fantastic progress.

"Trust you to keep me on the straight and narrow," he said, munching away, pointing at my signs.

Gran was pretty pleased too, even though she usually preferred me to take zero initiative when it came to helping out with the Granddad situation.

"Thank you, Cosmo, for the new signage system; that's such a kind thing to have done, isn't it, Kevin?" she said, and Granddad nodded with his mouth full, and Gran patted me on the head as if I were a kitten or a dog or something.

Later that night when I was helping to tuck him into his bed, he looked at me. His eyes had a paleness about them that I'd never seen before. "Bloody hell," he said. "Who are you?"

And I said, "Granddad, it's me. Can't you see it's me? Me, Cosmo."

"Well, hello, Cosmo. It's very nice to meet you. My name's Kevin, Kevin Lawless."

I pulled the duvet right up over his shoulders. I told him to try to get some sleep. He said he'd do his best.

Some people might think it would be depressing and miserable to live with people as old as my grandparents—all ticking clocks and hot chocolate and radio quizzes.

But it wasn't like that at all. Mostly it was excellent. They bought a big green lava lamp for my room, which made the light in there look wobbly and interesting, and when I told them the blankets on my bed were a bit scratchy, they immediately got me this huge soft white duvet and a whole load of green pillows. They said that this was my home now and I could bring my friends over whenever I wanted. I decided not to mention the fact that I didn't have any friends. I didn't want them to know that their only living grandson was a complete loner. They already had enough on their plates without having to worry about things like that.

My granddad did a lot of nice things for me, but the best thing of all was this: the exact same day I moved in, he drove off to a farm, and when he came back, he had a horse. He reckoned there was no sense keeping his money in the bank anymore.

"There's nothing quite like owning a horse to take your mind off your troubles," is what he said then, and he was right. If you take horse ownership seriously, you have lots of responsibilities, like feeding and exercising and foot care, so you can't waste your time worrying. Whenever I started to brood on anything, my granddad told me how the past is frozen, like ice, and the future is liquid, like water. And how the present is the freezing point of time.

"Make the most of the present," he said. "It's usually the only place in which you can get anything worthwhile done."

I still like to think about that sometimes. The entire human race—all of us—warriors of the present, every moment turning liquid future into solid past.

At first Granny Deedee was raging with Granddad about my horse. She asked him whether he had "utterly lost" his "marbles" and said that at the very least he should have consulted her. But he kept telling her that everything was going to be fine, and for a good while she kept believing him. We both did.

I'm not sure if I've mentioned it already, but the reason I had to move in with my grandparents was that my mum had to go to Sydney. It was something to do with how the market had dried up over here.

"At least she has her mobile phone," my gran had said cheerfully, just after Mum left. And I'd said, "Yeah, great, thank goodness for that."

Every time Mum called to say hi, I told Gran to let her know that I was a hundred percent fine. Gran would say, "Sweetheart, why don't you tell her yourself?" holding the phone out toward me like it was some kind of weapon. But I was usually too busy, to be perfectly honest. And anyway, you're rarely in the mood to talk to a person who goes off to Sydney when there are still loads of people over here who'd have found it sort of handy if she'd stayed where she was.

I don't mean to be nasty or anything, but I had begun to

think that my mum wasn't really a proper parent. Not only had she given me a fairly stupid name, she had also left me to cope with a lot of things that I shouldn't have had to deal with at all. I was only a kid. It wasn't fair. *I* didn't pack my bags and say I was leaving, however much I would have liked to. You don't take off like that just because times have gotten a bit rough. *I* happen to believe that when you have responsibilities, you should stick around.

I would have much preferred to keep my granddad's memory problems to myself, but it turns out that the guy I'd met at the train station was in my school. He told some of the people in my class about what he'd seen my granddad doing, and then those guys went around saying that my granddad was a psycho. They told everyone that he talked to lampposts and peed in public, which was true, but it sounded a lot worse the way they said it.

And then the whole entire school seemed to be in on the news that my granddad was a proper mental case, which was getting more and more difficult to disagree with.

You'd think that having a mental granddad might make people want to be slightly nice to you once in a while, but it doesn't work like that. D. J. Burke started to call me "Loser Boy." It's not like I cared what anyone thought about me—it was just that "Loser Boy" happens to be exactly the kind of name that is quite hard to get rid of, especially when D. J. Burke starts calling you it.

"Don't give him any oxygen," Granny Deedee said when I decided to tell her about it one night.

"Dee, that's the most ineffective advice you can give a boy in those kinds of circumstances," said Granddad.

I was thrilled. More proof that my granddad's brain was still working fine.

Granddad took me by the shoulders and looked at me with a load of focus and enthusiasm, and he said, "Bring that boy to the ground with all the energy you have. Stand on his chest and point your shoe toward his chin, and tell him that your will is greater than his. Keep him on the ground like that until he agrees not to call you names anymore. That should do the trick."

After my granddad was in bed, Gran said that I was not for a moment to consider taking that advice, and she explained that Granddad hadn't really been himself when he'd given it to me. I said that okay, I wouldn't, even though in my head I was thinking that it seemed like quite a good strategy. It felt like it would work much better than Granny Deedee's metaphorical oxygen-restricting guidelines.

Not long after that, D. J. spent an entire recess shouting, "Hey, Loser Boy," at me. He walked over and stood for about ten seconds staring very closely at my face and breathing quite loudly. Then he spat his bubble gum at me and pulled my bag off my back so that everything in it, like my compass and ruler and copies and pens, clanged and skidded and slid all over the floor of the corridor.

"Flip off," I said as he was walking away, but I may have said it quite quietly, because I don't think he heard.

"Cosmo, why does chaos appear to accompany you wherever you go?" asked Mrs. Cribben, my history teacher, who happened to be passing by. And I felt like telling her to flip off with herself as well. But in the end I didn't bother.

Later in class when Mrs. Cribben asked each of us what our special skill was, I said "riding."

The Geraghty twins both started to laugh in this identical way they have, showing off their oddly small teeth, and D. J. Burke did a mocking kind of snort until snot came out of his nose.

I didn't see what the problem with telling the truth was, even if it did sound hilarious to the three biggest idiots in my class.

My granddad had taught me all the things he knew about horses, including how to gallop really fast on them. It's a pretty difficult thing to do, but he always said I was a natural.

At least that's what he used to say until he forgot my name and started asking me who I was and what I was doing in his house.

It was excellent to be the owner of a horse, even though everyone kept having a huge convulsion about it because of the expense of renting the stables, but as far as I was concerned, it was well worth it because otherwise we wouldn't have had anywhere to keep him.

My horse's name was John. I took him out after school every single day. I used to shout in for Granddad as soon as I got home, and then he'd put on his coat while I threw my bag at the door. And Gran would stick her head out the window when we were already on our way.

"WHEN are you going to do your HOMEwork?"

Me and Granddad would both say, "Later," so that our voices sounded like we were one person, and then we'd walk down to the stables and Granddad would tell me that I was learning a million important things every time I went for a run with John—"Better than any homework," is what he used to say.

Granddad would look carefully at each one of John's feet, and he would trace his stump of an index finger around the grooves of John's shoes and feel every single one of the little bolts to make sure they were fine and tight. If there was even the slightest thing loose or frayed or wrong, then Granddad would replace the shoe, filing down any scraggy bits, because only by doing that can you be a hundred percent sure that your horse is going to stay sound. Granddad showed me how to do it in case, he said, there might be a day when he wasn't able to.

We'd carefully put his saddle and bridle on, and then my granddad would watch me as I jumped up. John was able to move extremely fast. He was a thousand percent better than a lot of humans I knew. For example, he never called me names or asked me nosy questions or got angry with me for being neurotic. Obviously. Because he was a horse.

Not everyone deserves to own a horse. It's not like having a Nintendo Wii or a skateboard or anything. People with short attention spans like most of the idiots in my class wouldn't have been able to take care of a horse in a million years. I mean, you can't throw them in the corner when you've finished with them. They are a massive responsibility.

Horses' feet are shaped like cups, and when they are galloping, the ridge of the cup connects with the ground and it expands ever so slightly to absorb the impact. So then the blood rushes to the horse's foot, which is exactly what the horse needs when he's running. Especially if there's a full-size human on his back.

If you keep a horse enclosed in wet conditions, then his feet can get all soggy, and if they get like that, they will eventually become horribly sore. If you change his shoes too often, then you can put too many nail holes in the rims of his hooves and wreck them. If you ever see a horse that's lame or limping, chances are that its owner didn't care enough about his feet.

Just by looking at the way a horse is standing, I can immediately tell you what's wrong and which foot needs attention and why, and I can file down parts of the rim of the hoof that have grown too much, and I can replace shoes or take off ones that are faulty.

Even though he was the expert horseman, Granddad said that I taught him a few things too. He said I was able to get horses to trust me. They never freaked out when I came near them.

He said that being worthy of trust is half the battle in life, no matter what it is that you're trying to do.

Me and John often galloped so fast that the people at the stables took stopwatches out. They told my granddad that I should definitely think about entering some of the competitions in my age group.

But we never wanted to win any prizes. Granddad didn't keep track of our progress or our speed or anything like that, no matter how often people kept saying that he should.

"When ambition lifts its nasty nose, joy creeps away," is what he used to say.

"What does that mean?" I asked him.

"It means that when you've found something that's worth doing for its own sake, you don't wreck it," he replied.

It was great when John and me were out there flying around the place. My granddad would watch us, as he leaned up against the fence, resting his chin on his arms with a smile on his gentle old face. We never knew how far we had galloped. We never knew how fast we had gone. It didn't matter. We just did it for the sake of it.

And when we were going really fast, I talked to John the way anyone might talk to someone who cared about them. I told him some of the mean things that people said to me, which was the kind of stuff I would have told Mum if she'd happened to be around at the time. I explained to him how Sydney, Australia, was roughly 17,420 kilometers away, and about what had happened to Brian—things that were hard to talk to anyone else about. I'm not saying he understood all the details or anything, but he definitely listened to me, unlike a lot of other people I know. As we thundered along, I sometimes whispered a song to him that my mum used to sing to me when I was smaller. I don't really know why, because it was all about seeing a baby for the first time and wanting to kiss the baby and relatively embarassing stuff like that, but I know he liked the sound of it. John was warm and strong and full of power. I always had this feeling, even when we were going very fast, that somehow he and my granddad were keeping me safe.

All the time we galloped around the place, Granddad would be proud and delighted-looking, with his cheeks getting lovely and red. After we'd finished, Granddad would help me hose John down and brush him. And then we'd feed him and settle him back in his stable, and me and Granddad would walk home.

I wanted it to be like that forever. The three of us hanging out together at the stables. But in the end Granddad couldn't come with me anymore. He tried his best and everything, but just because you try your best doesn't always mean you get superb results.

That last autumn was cold but it hardly ever rained as far as I remember, and by the time we'd finished, the light was always completely gone.

"I love the dark. I love the dark," he'd say as we walked home together under the evening sky.

"Yeah, I know, Granddad. You keep telling me," I'd say back.

But I understood what he meant. The dark is like a blanket, lying over the world, waiting to be pulled back so everything will be clear again.

Chapter 3

I KNOW THERE'S a recession and everything, but Australia? That's more or less the farthest away you can get. I bet Mum that there were new markets somewhere a bit closer than that, and she even said I was probably right. But anything Mum says doesn't count if she's checking e-mail on her cell phone when she's saying it. She'd been gone for ages. She'd said she'd be back in no time. I was beginning to think that "no time" was right. No time, as in never.

ACTION NUMBER 3: Make omega-3 fatty acids part of your loved one's daily nutrition plan.

Omega-3 oils contain all of the ingredients you need to help keep the brain strong. The best source is fish—smoked salmon is a handy staple to have in the fridge. It can be used in a wide range of snacks and healthy meals.

There was an excellent special offer in the supermarket, where you could buy two whole sides of smoked salmon in taped-together packets for ten ninety-nine. I took enough money out of Gran's bag to buy five packs, because it's not every day you come across money-saving offers like that.

The woman at the checkout wanted to know if I was having a party. It was none of her business. I just said yes, I was.

"Well, the best of luck with it," she said, and I said, "Yeah, right, thanks."

When Gran opened the fridge, about three of the packets fell out onto the floor, and she went ballistic, which is something she usually never does. She said I was no better than a thief, which was a total misrepresentation of the situation. She said I needed immediately to snap out of whatever behavioral issues I was in the middle of having, because she had enough to deal with already.

I made smoked salmon pâté from a recipe I got on the Internet, with lemon juice and pepper. It took me ages. "God bless the information age," said my granddad. He said that it was pretty much the most delicious thing he'd tasted in his whole life. Gran said that, funnily enough, she often used to make that *exact* same recipe many years ago, but that Granddad must have forgotten. She stood up, threw her napkin down on the chair, and walked really fast out of the room.

And then, as if there weren't enough tension in the house already, Granddad fell down the stairs. We had to call the ambulance, and me and Granny Deedee had to go with him to the hospital. It turned out he'd broken his leg. Granny Deedee gave the doctors a whole load of private information about Granddad and his recent behavior, which I knew straightaway was a mistake.

The people in the hospital lent us a wheelchair. The sun was coming up when we eventually brought Granddad home.

The very next day this woman called Dr. Sally arrived at our house with a few other people. I was standing by the living room window. I saw them coming. They parked up on the sidewalk, which is illegal, and whispered to each other as they walked toward our front door. My gran told me they were social workers.

Dr. Sally wore a clean, smooth white shirt with small transparent plastic buttons in the shapes of flowers. The first thing she did was tell me all about her own spectacular children and how one of them was the same age as me, as if I actually cared. She smiled practically all the time. There's no possible way that anyone could really be as permanently happy and delighted and thrilled as she seemed to be.

She kept asking these irrelevant nosy questions, like where I did my homework and how long my mother had been away, and what we did on the weekends and how many people came to visit us.

She pronounced all her words fantastically carefully, especially when she was talking to Granddad, whom she obviously mistook for some kind of an imbecile. And in fairness, Granddad wasn't really much help in my mission to get everyone to leave us alone. By then he had more or less stopped being able to do anything.

Dr. Sally said she was going to give Granddad "a little test."

"Who is this, Kevin? Who. Is. This?" she shouted at him, loud and slow, pointing her neat nail-polished finger at me. Granddad looked pale and vacant and said, "Thank you," which was obviously not the right answer.

"Stop it," I said to her. "You're stressing him out. Leave him alone. He knows who I am. Just because he's not telling you doesn't mean he doesn't know."

She kept saying, "All right, Cosmo. It's all right."

And she kept saying how heartbreaking it must have been for me to have to see my granddad suffering like this. But to tell you the truth, it didn't break my heart. It just embarrassed my brain, which is a different thing completely.

I never asked her if I could see a copy of her qualifications, though I should have. I never asked her for a search warrant, either, but I should have done that, too, considering all the prying and poking around she did. Dr. Sally sat down with Granddad and asked him a whole load of other questions, like who the president of America was and why was a carrot like a potato and what year did World War II start and what was his first ever job and how did he lose his finger.

My granddad looked down at his hand and went, "Good God! My finger! It's missing. Assemble a search party!"

"That's what he always says. It's a joke," I tried to explain, but I could see from the way she was scribbling everything down on her clipboard that she didn't think it was funny.

A few days after that, without warning, Uncle Ted came back from San Francisco.

Gran was delighted to see him, and she said he was looking marvelous, which was definitely not true. He had a massive peeling red nose and a leather bag dangling over his shoulder. When Gran went off to make tea, Ted looked straight into my granddad's face and he said, "Howerya, Dad?" but Granddad didn't happen to be in the mood for a conversation, which was totally his prerogative. Ted asked me what all the Post-its were for, but I didn't feel like explaining the whole thing to him. Eventually he said, "The signs are for Dad, aren't they, Cosmo?" like he thought he was some kind of detective, and I said, "Yeah. Who did you think they were for?"

Ted is a scientist. The way he talked about his work, you'd get the impression that he spent his whole life splitting atoms and growing human spleens from the ears of rats and stuff. But he was very uncreative when it came to problems closer to home. Ted told me that no one ever recovers from Alzheimer's, which is what he said my granddad had. I definitely wasn't going to accept that. Why should you take one person's word for it when there are approximately a thousand websites that say the complete opposite?

"Cosmo, you're interfering with the natural order of things," he said.

"Yes, well, what's wrong with that? If the natural order of things is as lousy as this, then it's my *responsibility* to interfere with it."

He sighed.

"Listen, you're going to have to adjust like the rest of us. There's no point. You have to accept it. There's nothing we can do to get his memory back."

"Shut up," I whispered. "His memory might not be that great, but his hearing's perfect."

And to prove it, as soon as the doorbell went, Granddad said I'd better get it because maybe this time it was Brian come back at last. And I said, "For the last time, Granddad, it's not Brian."

Chapter 4

IT WAS DR. SALLY again with the gang of social workers. They all clustered around our doorstep with their fake-friendly faces. Ted said he had wanted to have a bit of a chat with them to help us decide what was best for me and Gran, and that he'd gotten this so-called fabulous idea that involved him staying in Ireland permanently and renting a house down the road. And then he said that I could move in with him. He wanted me to start packing more or less straightaway. He also said he thought that we needed to start thinking of Granddad and about how he'd probably have to be moved to a place where he would be able to get full-time care.

"Eh, hello, sorry," I said. "In case you haven't noticed, that's exactly the kind of care he's already getting. Here with me and Gran."

Ted seemed genuinely amazed that I wasn't treating his plan as though it was the highlight of my entire life. He said it was time I started to grow up a bit and to realize that things don't stay the same forever, as if I didn't already know that. I think I might have thrown an empty teacup in his direction then. I can't exactly remember.

After that, Uncle Ted went a bit mad himself, and he started to say how one of my problems was that no one had ever taught me proper manners. He said I was being purposely difficult and extremely disrespectful, especially considering he'd rearranged his whole life for us. I told him that nobody had asked him to rearrange his stupid life.

Granny Deedee came in with a massive tray full of more cups of tea, as if that were the cure for everything.

My head felt a bit sore and I was sick of talking, so I locked myself in the bathroom. It felt good sitting on the cold floor with the door shut and nobody looking at me or asking me questions or telling me I was rude, but I knew I couldn't stay there forever.

By the time I came out, Dr. Sally was telling Granny Deedee how sometimes people need help even though they won't admit it, and Ted was wooden-faced, nodding his head, as though he was a puppet, not a fully grown human being.

Dr. Sally told me that my granddad was going to "rest quietly" at home tonight and that at the end of the week she'd come back to do the "little test" again when everything was a bit calmer. If he didn't pass it this time, they were going to take Granddad away to a nursing home.

"Gran?" I said, turning to her for a bit of support.

But she was in on the plan too. They all said I was going to be allowed to see him whenever I liked but that now I absolutely had to move in with my uncle Ted.

They said that I was allowed to go into my granddad's room to say good-bye, as if someone had to give me permission to go to a place where me and granddad hung out all the time reading books and chatting.

"Has anyone asked my granddad what HE wants?"

There was this big awkward silence.

"He wants to stay here and he wants me to stay here too. He doesn't want people coming and doing tests on him, and he doesn't need it. You've all got this whole thing a hundred percent wrong. There's nothing the matter with his brain."

"Cosmo, will you for God's sake calm down," said Ted.

I hate it when people tell me to calm down. It's basically one of the things I hate most in the world. And anyway, I *was* calm. I was thinking a lot more logically than most of the morons I was surrounded by.

"He's getting better. I've been doing this system with him, and it's working. I know it is."

None of them had ever heard of the Memory Cure website, even though it was established in 2005.

"You've got to stay up-to-date with the latest developments," I told them. "Otherwise you can't call yourselves professionals at all."

I made them stand around the computer, and I showed everyone.

"See? There are plenty of things you can do when someone gets forgetful—it's only a matter of trying."

"Oh, Cosmo, my love," was the completely useless thing that Granny Deedee said then. And she came over to me with her arms stretched out like a zombie, and then she gave me a hug, which was something I was not particularly in the mood for. She held me by my shoulders very gently and she said, "Darling, there are thousands of things in this world that we'll never be able to understand or control. There are things you have to accept, things you have to believe are happening for a reason, even if it's not something anyone can explain."

She loved saying things like that, about us not being able to understand things. And then she was all like, "Look, I know this has all been very difficult for you." She went on with the exact same kinds of things that Uncle Ted had said earlier, about "learning to accept" and "coming to terms" and "the natural order of things."

"Coming to terms" with something is another way of saying "giving up." I wasn't going to do that. I would never do that. And besides, action number four of the Memory Cure website said:

Negative thoughts are the enemies of brain health. Adopt a positive mental attitude at all times.

When I finally did go in to say good-bye, Granddad was lying on his side with both hands pressed together under his cheek.

His eyes were closed and he was snoring a little bit. I put my hand on his head.

"Granddad. Granddad. I'm really sorry, but I have to go. They think it's better if I stay with Uncle Ted for a while."

And it might sound a bit pathetic, but I kind of kept patting his head and I kept on not wanting to leave him. I didn't think he was going to wake up.

But then his eyes opened. He grabbed my hand very tightly and he looked at me, alert and bright and focused, and he whispered:

"Cosmo. It's you!"

I wanted to run out to them all. I wanted to shout, "SEE? See, everyone. He *knows* who I am. My system is working. He *hasn't* forgotten me."

I told him that I didn't want to leave, that I had planned to stay here with him and Gran.

My granddad used to say that the best way to make the gods laugh was to tell them your plans. He reminded me about that in his room that day, and then he chuckled away and I was sure then that he was going to get back to being his old self completely. But there wasn't time to go and explain it to anyone, because then he was saying something else:

"Listen to me, Cosmo. You must listen to me very, very carefully. There's something I have to tell you. Something important. I'm only going to say it once.

"Here's the thing: I know my mind is failing. And I know you've been doing your best, but there's only one thing that can help me now."

"What is it, Granddad?" I asked, my voice trembling a little bit.

"It's a key, Cosmo. It's going to help you find the answer to everything, and I'm going to give it to you. You're the only person I could possibly trust with it. You must promise to use it carefully. It's a key to the gates."

"What gates?"

"The south gates."

"The south gates of what?"

"Of the Abbey."

"What abbey?"

"Blackbrick Abbey, of course."

He reached his brown twisted hand over to a small box that had always, as far as I could remember, sat on his bedside table. He fumbled and scrabbled around a bit before he opened the box and took something out.

"Here," he said, holding up this small, gray, dented thing. It took a good bit of looking carefully at it before I realized it must've been the key he'd been talking about.

"Open the gates with it. Make sure you lock them behind you as soon as you're on the other side. It would never do to let anyone else in, do you hear me? Blackbrick. South gates. Do you understand, Cosmo? Do you understand completely?"

I didn't understand. Not even partially. But I nodded and tried to make my face look reassuring and calm.

"There'll be nothing to worry about, because guess what?" he said.

"What?"

He lowered his voice. I had to lean in really close to hear.

"I'll be there. On the other side. Waiting for you. Bring a pen and paper. That's what you'll need to do, that's a good fellow. Promise me you'll go."

It felt like someone had punched me in the stomach. It was proof that he really had lost it—that he really was a psycho, just like everybody kept saying.

The Memory Cure website's action number five said:

Never act surprised or confused about what your loved one says. Always behave as if you know what they're talking about, even if what they're saying appears strange or incoherent.

I said, "Okay, okay, I will, I'll go there," even though I knew that I probably wouldn't.

"Well done. Excellent," he said, smiling. "I knew you wouldn't let me down."

I took the key from him, and I said, "Thanks."

Thanks a bloody million.

Chapter 5

EVERYONE WAS waiting when I came out. Ted was smiling, and the social workers' heads were bobbing up and down enthusiastically and they were saying things like, "Well done, Cosmo, good man," as if this was supposed to be the best day of my life and I should have been delighted.

"Don't worry!" said Dr. Sally as though she was about to explode with joy. "You'll be in good hands!"

"Am I still going to be able to go to the stables after school?"

And that was when Ted said, "Oh yes, sorry, em, about that, we forgot to tell you. We have to send John away. He's going to a farm. In the country. Where he can run around all day and be happy."

"A FARM in the COUNTRY?" I shouted. "What do you think I am, SIX? I know what that means. You're going to have him put down. That's basically MURDER."

"Cosmo. I promise we're not doing that."

He gave me the phone number of the farm and said I could call and talk to them about John to prove that he wasn't having him killed.

Dr. Sally told me that I should try to think about what my gran was feeling, and that it would be a good thing for me to think of other people for a change, and I told Dr. Sally to shut up and go away and never come back. She definitely heard me. It was the first time since I'd met her that she stopped smiling.

I called the farm in the country. They said I could come and visit John whenever I wanted, but it turns out that "the country" was Kildare, which is miles away. Even though I'm not the most practical person in the world, I already knew the logistics were going to be a nightmare.

Nothing was ever going to be the same.

I gave the farm person on the other end of the phone a load of instructions about how they should take care of John and what he liked to eat and how to brush him and how warm his stable should be and how to look after his feet, which are the most important thing of all you need to focus on when you're in charge of a horse. I asked them if they were writing it down, because it was a lot to remember.

After a while I did calm down a bit, but it was just because I was tired.

I spent a long time looking at the ceiling of Ted's spare room that night, thinking about John and about the mad promise I'd made to my granddad.

You shouldn't break the promises you make to people. Nobody should. You can't go around saying you promise to do something and then not do it. Even if you're pretty much certain that the thing you have promised to do is for the birds.

I lay still on the bed the whole time, turning the little key that Granddad had given me over and over in my hand until it was hot. I waited until everything was quiet and there were no bumps or murmurs or clicks coming from anywhere. Then I slid off the bed, and I inched my way downstairs very quietly. Hanging off the back of a chair in the kitchen was Ted's bag. Inside it I found a notebook with a hard black cover, a few pens, and a wallet full of fifties and twenties. I crammed everything back in, grabbed the whole bag, and called a taxi.

The taxi guy came pretty quickly. He wasn't that talkative, but he knew where Blackbrick Abbey was, which was the first relief of that particular day. Soon we were on roads that I'd never been on before, all twisty and black.

When silence grows in a small space, it gets harder and harder to say anything at all. For example, there were loads of times on that journey when I wanted to tell the taxi guy to turn back. I needed to ask Granddad what the heck he had meant and why, out of the complete blue, he'd wanted me to go to a place that I'd never heard of in my whole life, and why it was suddenly so important that he'd made me promise. But I wasn't able to speak. Ages of time went by, and the taxi guy kept on driving, and it kept on getting darker and foggier. I started feeling quite stupid.

It didn't help that the taxi smelled as if someone had thrown up in it. For a while I thought I was going to throw up myself.

But then there was an old black gate with stone pillars on either side and forbidding walls, and in part of the wall were carved tall letters. It was so shadowy that first I could only see a big *B*, but as we got closer, I saw that the *B* was only the beginning and that the whole sign did say BLACK-BRICK ABBEY. The huge crumbly black gates were closed and locked. Behind them was the beginning of what looked like a massive driveway covered in brown shiny gravel.

"Anywhere here is fine, thank you," I said, even though anywhere there was not fine at all.

I uncurled my hand and looked at Granddad's key.

I got out. Taxi Guy was sitting there waiting for me to pay, his big fat elbow resting saggily on the open car window. I felt lousy and on my own, and my heart had started to gallop around. It was something to do with the way the air smelled. Something to do with the sounds of the massive big trees that were creaking like hundreds of old doors opening very slowly, and it was also a little bit to do with the whistling of the wind through the black branches. But it was mainly to do with being in the middle of nowhere in the middle of the stupid night.

"Em, listen," I said. "Can you take me back, please?"

"Back where?" he asked, looking kind of amazed.

"You know, back to where you picked me up."

"Sorry. No can do," he replied. "I've gone out of my way already."

"Out of your WAY?" I said. "Stop me if I'm wrong, but isn't that the whole POINT of driving a stupid TAXI?"

"Calm down, mate," he said. "There's no need to be rude."

As well as hating it when people tell me to calm down, I hate it even more when someone I don't know calls me "mate," especially if I've never met them before and it's obvious that they don't even like me. I paid him what I owed him, which was thirty-seven fifty, and then I pulled out another twenty. I kept my voice steady, and I said to him, "Okay, listen. I need you to give me fifteen minutes. That's all. If I'm not back by then, you can go."

He sucked some air in through his nose for a second or two, calculating something in his head.

"All right, then," he said, snatching the money with impressive skill and transforming it into a crumpled blur as he slid it into his pocket. Then he took a newspaper from under his seat, and it crinkled as he spread it out over the dashboard. "Fifteen minutes. But that's it. I'm not waiting any longer than that."

I could feel a draft of cold air creeping into my body as I walked toward the gates. I was going to keep my promise to Granddad. It's not like I was going to stay very long or anything. I thought it would be okay to have a quick look around the place. And then I was going to go back to Ted's before anyone had even noticed I was gone. And next time I saw my granddad, I was going to try to explain to him how I'd done what he had asked. That I'd kept my promise. And that was going to be that.

A massive old padlock hung, dead and heavy, from a bolt where the two gates joined, all caked with knobbles and flakes of rust. It took ages of pulling and twisting. Finally I loosened the padlock and dragged it toward me. It looked as though nobody had opened it for a very, very long time.

I felt around for the keyhole and wiggled Granddad's key into it. At first it didn't look like it was going to work. I was standing in the night with fog all around me and Granddad's key stuck in the padlock now, and I couldn't twist it or move it in any direction, and I couldn't pull it out. I looked back. I could see Taxi Guy lit in a dim orange glow inside his car, reading the paper, not caring about me or anything else, as far as I could see.

I shook the gates backward and forward, and they made a heavy, low clanking noise.

"Where have you sent me? Where am I?" I shouted, and the sound of those questions went floating into the black sky. I cursed myself for being brainless enough to have gone to so much trouble, only to find myself in this empty, cold place. But what else did I expect?

I was just about to turn away, when there was a little crack. The padlock sprang open.

I stopped breathing for a few seconds, pulled the padlock off, and slid the bolt across. It took another huge amount of effort, and my hands got covered in rust, which was gross.

I pushed the gates forward, and the entrance opened like an enormous toothy mouth doing a slow yawn. Small clusters of gravel piled up at the bottom on either side. I walked through and I closed and locked the gates again, just as Granddad's mad instructions had specified, and I shoved the key into my pocket.

It was Monday night. Ted was probably going to be up early in the morning to kick me out of bed for school. I hadn't done any homework because of the traumatic events of the day, so I seriously wasn't planning to stick around for too long.

I couldn't see much. A tiny low wreck of a cottage sat tucked away to the right, but there was no light or sign that there was anyone living there. The driveway looked as if it led to something much bigger, the way it widened and curved and stretched off into the distance.

And then out of the quiet foggy air came a rustle from the trees to the left, and I knew someone was there even before I could see them. The trees parted for a second as if somebody was pushing them to one side, and that's because somebody was, and then the somebody was walking toward me and all I could hear was the echoey *crunch* of their feet stamping on the gravel.

For a while I thought I was going to fall. I wouldn't have

been that surprised if I'd lost consciousness, because in fact you can only get so nervous before you pass out. I saw shadows and I smelled the foggy smell of night there inside the gates of Blackbrick.

And I saw his gradually brightening shape coming toward me.

It was a boy. And soon he was standing, strong and tall on top of this low wall beside the trees, right in front of me with his hands on his hips and his legs wide apart, and there was a soft-looking frown on his young smooth face.

"How did you get in here?" he asked me.

"I've got a key to these gates. I just opened them up," I said.

"But it's the middle of the night. No one ever uses those gates. They've been locked for a long time. What are you doing here?"

I tried to keep my voice steady.

"I was only having a look around. I have permission. At least I wasn't hiding behind a bunch of trees and giving people massive heart attacks like you were."

"I live here. I've got a right to be here," said the boy. "This is where I work."

"Yeah, well, that still doesn't explain what you were doing, hiding in the trees like that, here in the dark."

"I love the dark," he said.

I blinked a few times and looked at him very carefully then.

"Now, tell me," he said, "who on earth are you?"

He held out his hand, and that's when I could feel my skin tightening all over, and it felt like my body had suddenly become too small to contain all the things that were in me. I could feel a ridge rising all the way along my back as if I were a dog. Because he wasn't pointing, not the way most people are able to. There was something pretty noticeable about the finger he should have been pointing with.

It was missing.

Chapter 6

"WOW," I whispered.

He put his hand down again, and he looked at me staring at his absent finger.

"Listen here, whoever you are, I might be short a finger, but there are worse things you could be missing, when you think about it."

His eyes were clear and wrinkle-free, and there were no red veins in them and they weren't watery.

"Wa HA!" My voice went floating into the sky again. "Granddad, you DID it! It's really true, and I thought it was because you were losing your marbles, but you weren't! You're a genius! I always knew it, and now here's the proof! You've made a bloody portal! Ha! You've done it. And it WORKS. You gave me the key, and here I am, and here you are.

"You're, like, a million times better than Albert Einstein or Stephen Hawking. You didn't need any flux capacitors or TARDISes or cosmic strings or gravitational laser solutions. YOU did it with this one tiny key. I always knew it, Grand-dad. You really are the cleverest guy I ever met. I just didn't realize you were able to do time travel. But you a hundred percent ARE."

By then I was jumping around, and all these things were kind of dancing in my brain, mainly about how everything was going to be fine now that I was here. I would be able to tell him a whole load of important things that he should know, like, for example, about Brian falling out the window, and the value of getting into good brain-health habits as soon as possible so he wouldn't lose his memory when he got older. Everything was possible again. Everything was going to be grand.

Prevention is always a million percent better than cure. Everybody knows that.

"What are you talking about?" he said. "I never gave you any key, and you're not to go around telling anyone I did. Now, it would be more in your line to stop with your nonsense talk and tell me what your name is."

"It's me. It's me, Cosmo!" I said.

"I'm not prepared to listen to lies. I'd ask you please to tell me the truth."

"I *am* telling it," I said.

But he said I couldn't possibly be, because for one thing there wasn't anybody in the world who had a name anything like "Cosmo."

He was backing away from me the way someone does when they've come face-to-face with something dangerous or bizarre or mad.

And then I could hear my voice trailing off into a thin little thread the way someone's voice does when he's just realized that a brilliant situation might not in fact be that brilliant after all.

He was shaking his head.

He swiped his hand through his hair.

"All right," he said. "Let's get this straight: I haven't the foggiest notion who you are. But whoever you do happen to be, I am definitely not your granddad. I'm nobody's granddad. I'm Kevin. Kevin Lawless. I'm sixteen."

He breathed in, and the fog crept up into his nose.

Even though his voice was gentle, he definitely thought I was the greatest nutter that had ever lived. I wasn't stupid. I could see that.

"There's not many who would believe a story like the one you're trying to tell me," he said.

"I know . . . I guess . . . I mean, I suppose it would sound kind of strange if you weren't expecting it," I said.

"Yes. It would," he said.

"Okay, then. Please listen." I walked toward him, holding my arms out in front of me, but he backed away even farther then.

"Hold on, steady now," he replied. "Keep your distance if you don't mind."

The whole time I couldn't stop thinking how young he looked and how strong he was and how he had whole big decades of his life still in front of him. Years and years and years that he hadn't even started to live.

Very few people ever get to see their grandparents like that. Not even in their imaginations.

Neither of us said anything for more or less ages. We kept staring at each other, until I whispered: "You really don't have a clue who I am, do you?"

And just as quietly he said, "No, sir. I don't."

It didn't make a difference which stupid time zone I was in. Granddad Kevin didn't know me in either of them.

You don't have to be recognized by every single person you've ever met. Wanting that would be egotistical. But there are one or two people in your life who should always know who you are. You'll probably never know how important that is unless one of those people starts to forget you.

I sat down on the wall. I'm not a hundred percent sure, but I might have started crying a bit. He came over then and sat beside me. The wall was kind of damp, and we looked up at the stars, which were bright and twinkling even though the cold fog still moved, like the ghosts of snakes, in between the trees and around our feet.

He took a big crumpled white cloth out of his pocket and he handed it to me. I blew my nose.

"Good man, that's it," he said.

He sounded as if he was trying to cheer me up, the way you might if you wanted to stop a very small child from being sad or lonely or scared. I didn't need him to feel sorry for me. I didn't like him thinking I was the world's most pathetic loser.

"Are you all right?" he asked, and it sounded as though he really cared.

I sniffed, and I said, "Yeah, I'm grand, don't worry about me."

We got to chatting. I asked him what kind of work he did in this place.

He told me that he worked in the stables. He said that he was learning to be a farrier, but that the person who was teaching him had gone off to the war, like a lot of people who used to work here, and he wasn't sure when he was going to be back. He started explaining that farriers were people who fix and mend and mind horses' feet, as if I didn't already know that.

I told him that, as a matter of fact, I had a lot of equine-related skills myself, and he said, "Is that right?"

And I said that yes, it was.

And he asked me had I ever shod a horse, and I said I was practically an expert.

He asked me was I a good rider. I said I wasn't bad.

He wondered if I knew how to attach horses to a cart, and I admitted that I didn't. But I told him that I was very good at talking to horses and keeping them calm and getting them to trust me, and he said, "Well, that's half the battle, no matter what you're trying to do."

We were quiet then for a few minutes.

I told him I'd better go home because there wasn't much point in sticking around. There were millions of things I wanted to tell him—important advice that would make a massive difference to us all, but I couldn't really think of a way of saying it without sounding like even more of a weirdo than he'd already taken me for. I told him I was sorry for trespassing and that I hadn't meant to cause any trouble. He said it was nice to meet me, and I said, "Yeah, right, thanks."

I started walking toward the gates. But I could feel my heart getting cold because I knew the bizarre chance that I was walking away from. So I stopped walking and I turned. My young granddad was still looking at me.

"Listen, maybe I could stay for a little while," I suggested. "I mean, only for a few days. And maybe we could hang out."

He asked me what "hang out" meant, and I told him it meant spending time together, talking and suchlike. And for a while he didn't say anything, and I thought my chance was going to disappear, so then I did my best to think on my feet.

I said, "Is there anything that I could help you with, would you say?" It turns out that that's quite a good question to ask someone who doesn't trust you yet.

"Well, you know, in actual fact, now that you say it . . . yes. Yes, there is."

We were both shivering by then because a wind had

started to blow, and it was making the trees shudder, and it was getting harder to hear each other.

"Come with me," he said.

I followed him, and his feet were solid and strong and we ran up the driveway, and again I could hear the crunch of his footsteps. They sounded like the beating of someone's heart.

Chapter 7

IT'S NOT as though I'd forgotten about my old grandparents and Uncle Ted, and it's not like I wasn't worried about how mental they were definitely going to go when they got up the next morning and nobody could find me. Fifteen minutes was well up. The enchanted taxi guy of delight with the brilliant people skills had probably gone ages ago anyway, with the money in his pocket. There was a while there when I thought I probably should've run back to tell him I'd gotten a bit delayed. But when you find yourself seventy years or so out of your normal time zone, you're not necessarily thinking too straight.

Blackbrick Abbey was like a house, only much, much bigger. It sat at the end of the driveway, looking like it was more or less growing out of the ground. A shiny black door twinkled in a huge stone doorway, and there were steps leading up to it that glinted and flashed. My young granddad walked past the steps and tiptoed along a path that twisted its way around to the back. He kept looking over his shoulder, checking that I was still there. We crept through a small archway, shady and gray. Leaning from the wall, a weak flickering lamp lit the way.

"Stay close, move quickly, be quiet."

I did stay very close and I did move quickly and I was very quiet. We went in through another door. This one was squeaky and warped. And once we were in, everything smelled of smoke and leather. I followed him down all these ramshackle corridors.

We walked and walked for ages, and it got warmer the whole time until we were in this big cave of a kitchen. There was a massive table in the middle that at least twenty people could have sat around. There were big jars on counters in rows with labels on them saying FLOUR and SUGAR and OATS and GOOSEBERRY PRESERVES and stuff like that. Tons of wooden spoons stuck out of blue-and-white stripy pots, huge saucepans hung from pegs on the wall, and a load of sacks, full of potatoes, were lined up in one corner on the black stony floor.

He dragged a couple of chairs beside a gigantic hot stove. He leaned down to a wide bucket and he picked up rocks of coal, and then with an iron bar he lifted a round disc on top of the stove and an orange glow shone out of the hole, and he threw the bumpy, fist-size lumps into it. Then he clapped his hands together. A black cloud hovered around him for a second.

There was a huge kettle that my young granddad had to lift with both hands to put on the stove. The tea he made was strong and brown, and when he took a sip, he sighed and said, "Ah, fantastic."

Being a stable boy at Blackbrick was the first job he ever had. They'd taken him out of school when he was young so he could help take care of the horses. I told him that was the most excellent thing that could probably happen to anyone.

He said that the only reason I thought that was because I didn't know how much work was involved, especially now that all the farriers had gone off to the war.

I pulled Ted's black notebook out of the bag and asked my young granddad if I could take a few notes as long as it was okay with him. He said I could if I wanted, it was all the same to him.

And the whole time I started to warm up. It was mainly because of the stove and the tea. But it was also because of how I knew I was going to be able to give my old granddad a full briefing when I got back home, where he needed to be reminded about a few things, and he'd definitely pass Dr. Sally's test and would be able to stay at home with me and my gran. All I had to do was keep my head and remember everything, and not panic and try not to think about how weird the whole situation was.

"So, you want to help me?"

"Yes," I said, "I do."

"Well, that's grand, because there's an errand that I've been wanting to run for quite some time, and it requires getting out of here on two horses and a cart someday soon and then coming back, without anyone knowing.

Would you be interested in giving me a hand with that?"

It sounded pretty easy, so I said, "Sure, no problem at all."

And then he was delighted, like someone who was realizing something that they hadn't realized before. He shook my hand and kept saying, "Well, sir, that's good news. Thank you, sir. Thank you very much indeed."

I told him that he didn't have to call me "sir" or anything like that. I told him that we were equal. I said I didn't want to get anyone into trouble with this plan and that I hoped he had thought the whole thing through as carefully as possible.

According to him there was nothing to worry about. Even though what we were going to do might seem a bit illegal, in actual fact it was an extremely good deed I was getting involved in. Apparently there was a person who needed a break because the person had about a million brothers and sisters whose parents could barely afford to feed them all, and the person would be much better off here at Blackbrick Abbey, where there was food and a lot more room.

I told him it sounded as if whoever this guy was, he was in a pretty socioeconomically disadvantaged situation. I said that it sounded like a very good idea to help him out.

And Kevin said, "It's not a him. She's a girl, and I'm bringing her here to Blackbrick. And now that you're prepared to assist me, there's nothing to stop us from going tomorrow. Tomorrow after my chores are done."

"A girl?"

"Yes, a girl. *The* girl. The girl I'm going to marry."

He was only sixteen years old, which was pretty young to be talking like that, but at the time I didn't care, because I could feel a thrill rippling through me. It didn't take a genius to figure out that he was obviously talking about my own gran, Granny Deedee. And it was exciting to think that I was going to meet her, too. I knew that as soon as I did, things were going to take a massively brilliant turn for the better. The much, much better.

My gran was the one who was always saying how there are things in life that we can't understand. She was the one who had this theory about there being so much in this world that we have to believe, even if we can't explain it. And I knew for sure that if I met her here, she would definitely believe me when I told her who I was, and when she did, everything was going to be a hundred percent grand.

That night Kevin showed me around my bedroom, which took about two and a half seconds, seeing as all there was in it was a bed and a chair. He picked up a limp pillow and started gently wrestling with it. He said he hoped I'd be comfortable. The chances of that looked quite slim, but still I said thanks.

I told him it had been a very confusing day. He said he'd be in the next room if I needed him but that I should try to get some sleep and maybe things would make more sense in the morning. I said nothing was probably going to make sense ever again in my whole life.

He asked me if I'd had any upsetting experiences recently, and I said, "I guess that's what you could call them."

He said, "I think that as soon as you have any distressing or strange thoughts, it's always the best thing to put them right out of your head."

He asked me to remind him what my name was again, and I said it was Cosmo. And he said, "No, honestly, what's your real name?" and I said seriously, that really was it. He said, "All right, then. Good night. See you in the morning."

Even though I was dog-tired, it was pretty hard to fall asleep. I don't reckon anyone would be able to go to sleep that easily after a) they'd just found out they were a time traveler who'd b) met their granddad when he was young, and c) were then trying to sleep on an extremely uncomfortable mattress in a very cold room.

There was a crack under the door, and I could hear Kevin still loitering outside, whistling, soft and low. And there was a whooshing noise that was possibly his feet dragging along the flagstones. I heard these clickety footsteps too, coming quite fast, closer and closer. They stopped, and a woman's crackly voice said, "Kevin! Goodness but this is a very late hour of the night for you to be up." And he said, "I know. I've been waiting to talk to you." And then he said, "There's something I need to tell you about." And Crackly said,

"What could you need to be telling me that couldn't wait till the morning?" and Kevin explained all about how he'd found this strange boy on the grounds and now the strange boy was asleep in the spare servant's room.

There was a pause, and I held my breath because it was a bit hard to hear everything.

"And how in the name of God did he get onto the grounds?"

"He had a key. A key to the south gates."

"Holy Saint Joseph, well, that's certainly a surprise," said Crackly. "I didn't think there was a single soul who had a key to those gates anymore."

"Neither did I," said Kevin. "And you see, the thing is that the fellow seems a bit unhinged. He had a daft story. Didn't seem to want to leave once he'd met me. Was in what you might call a bit of a state. I thought the best thing was to get him to calm down and put him to bed."

"Oh dear. Didn't you know that every stray boy you meet these days is madder than a brush? Gracious me, but will you ever learn? And you know you're not supposed to linger around those south gates. You know how upset everyone gets. What do you think Lord Corporamore would say? And why didn't you tell me?" she said.

"I'm telling you now, aren't I?" he replied.

The crackly voice laughed and said, "Yes, well, I suppose there's no arguing with that."

He went on a bit more about me then, all about how I

looked like I could do with a chance to "steady" myself, and that maybe this was my place of temporary refuge. But he didn't say a single thing about me helping him to bring my young gran into Blackbrick.

It wasn't the best feeling in the world to hear them talking away to each other about how nuts I was. I had enough people in my life who thought I was the world's biggest lunatic.

I'd say anyone who's done any time traveling would probably tell you that it's more or less the best opportunity you can possibly have to reinvent yourself. But in my case, within the space of less than a single night, he obviously already thought I was a loser.

"I suppose we could put him to work to earn his keep," said the voice, which had continued to soften under Kevin's clever manipulation. "A bit of extra help would come in fierce handy even if it's only for a few days."

And he said yes, he supposed it would. She told Kevin that on second thought he was very kind and compassionate to have put himself out for a stranger, and how goodness knows everyone deserves to be treated with kindness no matter who they are.

I pulled the blanket over my head and I started to wonder about a few things like, for example, what my gran was going to look like when she was young. And I also wondered what Ted was going to do when the sun came up and he realized I was gone, and whether or not he'd tell my old

Granny Deedee and the middle-aged Dr. Sally. Either way, I reckoned I'd probably be in trouble for pretty much the rest of my life.

The crackly voice trailed away then and so did Kevin's, and the low glow under the door disappeared. I didn't feel like I was going to, but after a while I must have fallen asleep.

Next thing it was early in the morning and thin wisps of light were starting to weave their way around the darkness, and clatters and noises were echoing from down the corridor into my room, and I could tell that someone was making breakfast.

Even when things don't make any sense at all and you're feeling very strange, I've often noticed that there is one smell that can be quite comforting, and that is the smell of toast.

Chapter 8

IT WASN'T only the toast, though. I was already picturing myself explaining everything to my young gran, and I was predicting how me and Kevin and her were all going to have this massive three-way hug and how it was going to be a million percent brilliant. For the first time in a long time, even though it was something like six a.m., I was looking forward to getting out of bed.

Kevin legged it into the room a few minutes later, saying good morning and pulling the thin curtains along their squeaky rails. "Would you like to come along with me while I do my morning chores?" he said.

I said, "Are you sure you really want to hang out with someone as unhinged as me?"

"I don't mind, as long as you keep up, because I move reasonably fast."

I told him I'd already noticed.

So next thing we were back in the kitchen and I was getting introduced to this woman, and she opened her mouth and the crackly voice came out.

"Welcome to Blackbrick," she said. "I'm Mrs. Kelly."

She also said that she'd agreed not to ask any more questions about me, even though creeping into someone's estate late at night is "fierce suspicious," and not exactly the way to do things. But as long as I was willing to do a few jobs around the place, she wasn't going to pry. Times were tough, she said, but she seemed to be pretty cheerful all the same.

"We're doing our best to get on with things, aren't we, Kevin? We're not griping about anything, sure we're not, Kevin, much and all as the temptation to complain sometimes grabs hold, God forgive me."

She was old, maybe forty. And she was big and her hands were pink and she had a very clean apron on. And when she sighed, the apron rose on her chest like a huge white wave.

"Now come on in and sit down for a bit."

She kept on looking at me quite carefully, like she was expecting me to make some wrong or possibly dangerous move, but she was very polite, and she said how she had to tell me the truth, which was that it was a good slice of luck to have another strong boy on the premises, even if it was only for a short stay. She said Blackbrick was once well known for taking very good care of its visitors, and that herself and Kevin would do their best to keep that reputation going even though it was going to be difficult, seeing how there were no other servants there anymore.

"If there's anything you need, all you have to do is ask, she said."

"Grand, no problem, thanks a lot."

The first thing Kevin had to do that morning was sweep a whole load of floors. He said that Mrs. Kelly was right about it being handy to have a bit of help for a change. He told me that there used to be more than twenty-five servants at Blackbrick: maids and stable boys and a cook and a butler and farriers and suchlike. Now there was only him and Mrs. Kelly, rattling around having to do all sorts of jobs they'd never have done in the old days. "The Emergency" was on, and not only had a load of the men gone off to fight in the war, but also Lord Corporamore had used the whole situation as an excuse to fire a load more because he was broke.

I told Kevin this was much earlier than I was used to getting up and that my blood sugar levels felt a bit low, but all he did was hand me a broom.

Sweeping a floor is actually not that bad an activity. To tell you the truth it comes with a good bit of job satisfaction—seeing something that has been dusty getting clean and clear just because you drag a broom across it.

After a while this enormous clock in the hall started clanging away, and Kevin said, "Oh, drat. Cordelia's breakfast."

It turned out that Cordelia was a Corporamore, and even though she was only a kid, like around eleven or something, anyone who was a Corporamore had to be obeyed, no matter how young they were. Kevin was meant to get breakfast ready for her at exactly eight o'clock every morning. And even though it would have been "most irregular" for a boy like Kevin to bring breakfast to any of the Corporamores in the old days, now there was no one else to do it except for Mrs. Kelly, who was working her fingers to the bone and whose bad knee made climbing the stairs to Cordelia's room pure torture. So Cordelia was waiting for breakfast, and apparently it was extremely important that Kevin was never late.

We sprinted to the kitchen, and Kevin fried five slices of bacon. He gave me one—it tasted pretty nice. He curled one into his own mouth and chewed, closing his eyes and humming for a second at the deliciousness of it. Then he put the other three onto two pieces of buttered toast. He stirred creamy scrambled eggs in a pan on the stove and tumbled them out onto a plate. Then he spooned jam into a little carved glass container, quickly and carefully arranging everything on this massive hard-to-carry tray.

He made sure that the knife and fork and spoon were all perfectly straight and that the napkin was folded in this precise way, as if he was someone with a serious case of OCD. He saw me staring at him. He explained that it had to be exactly like that every morning. If he didn't want Cordelia to become very out of sorts, he needed to be sure that he had everything arranged perfectly.

"She sounds pretty demanding," I said. He said I should come on up with him so I could see for myself.

So I followed him along more creaking hallways with faded pictures and dusty mirrors hanging on the walls. We stood outside another closed door. Kevin organized his face into a new expression, smiley and round-eyed and exaggerated. He knocked gently at first, but he didn't get any answer. He banged a bit harder.

"WHAT DO YOU WANT?" said this little skinny piercing kind of a voice from the other side, even though the person whose voice it was must have known.

"Miss Cordelia, your breakfast," he said.

"Oh, for goodness' sake, come IN, will you?" she whined.

"Stay here," Kevin whispered to me, and he shoved the door open with his shoulder and left me standing in the corridor, with paintings of people in ancient clothes gazing down at me.

I could hear him saying good morning and being fabulously polite.

In all the time I'd known my Granddad Kevin, which was my whole life, he'd never said anything about Blackbrick and he'd never once mentioned that he had been a slave. I personally think he should have told me important things like that.

The voice was the voice of the highest-maintenance kid in the history of the world.

"*You* were supposed to be here at eight o'clock," she said.

"Yes, Miss Cordelia. I'm sorry."

"What's taken you so long?"

"Well, I've had quite a lot to do."

"Well, *I* really must tell my father how useless you are. You're always late. You never do my breakfast the way I like it."

"I know," he said. "I'm sorry, Miss Cordelia."

All Kevin did was apologize and agree, and agree and apologize, and then he backed out of the room kind of bowing, like someone with zero self-esteem.

"You shouldn't let anybody talk to you like that," I said when we were back in the kitchen drinking tea. But according to him it was part of his job to let her talk whatever way she wanted, and anyway he said he didn't really take much notice. According to him there were advantages to being on Cordelia's breakfast duty. For one thing, you got to swipe a few slices of bacon. And that was quite handy because of it being in the middle of the war. There were massive food shortages, leading to quite a restricted supply of basic foodstuffs. And anyway, he said that as soon as he'd brought up that stupid tray to her and put up with her whining, by far the worst part of his day was over.

He was right. After that it was kind of a great day. The whole time I kept on thinking that very soon I'd be coming face-to-face with my granny Deedee. And I hummed away to myself all through the polishing and sweeping and cleaning and dusting and vegetable preparation.

And before long it was time to go to the stables. He told me it was a famous place. He said that twelve horses used to live there, but now that everything was being cut back, there were only two left.

The paint on the stable doors was split and peeling.

There was hay and sawdust and pieces of flat wood under-foot that cracked and snapped as we walked along, and the horses made these warm, low, muffled noises of welcome, and I could feel something going all calm inside me. Kevin opened the stable doors and led the horses into the court-yard. Their backs were sleek and shiny, and they nodded their lovely heads and Kevin said, "Shh, shh, you two. I want you to meet someone." He talked to them as if they were people. "This fellow's name is Cosmo."

I reached out my hands and stroked their noses.

"This is Somerville." Kevin patted her neck. "And this is Ross," who was the bigger of the two.

I put my cheek up against Ross's face and my hand on Somerville's strong shiny back, and we stayed like that for ages standing very still, breathing in and out.

Eventually Kevin said we'd better get on with things. I looked down and lifted one of Ross's legs, and Kevin lifted one of Somerville's, and in exactly the same way I traced my fully intact finger and he traced his stump of one around the grooves, and we both felt the little bolts to make sure they were fine and tight.

There was something magic about us doing exactly that same thing at exactly the same time like that, and I think he noticed it too.

"Who are you, Cosmo?" he asked.

"I thought I wasn't allowed to talk about that anymore," I replied.

"Fair enough, then," he said, and he smiled and looked down again at the horses' feet.

Hitching horses to a cart is a difficult thing to do, especially when there's not much light left and there are only two people available to do it, and one of them doesn't know how to, but I watched him really carefully and tried to remember everything.

"I thought you said you were a horseman," said Kevin. He reckoned it was weird that I didn't know anything about carts. I said nobody learns everything all in one go.

Afterward I drew a few sketches and wrote all the details down in Ted's notebook because you never know when information like that will be useful.

I did my best not to think too much about the present, but it wasn't easy. It kept floating into my head in the middle of conversations with Kevin, and I kept picturing John and wondering how he was getting on in his new home and thinking about how much I needed to see him. But I was committed to spending at least a few days in the past, and okay, it was weird that I was there and everything, but I had to stay calm, and I had to keep it together. When I did think about what Ted and Granny and Granddad might be doing now that I was probably an official missing person, I started to feel sick. I just hoped that when I got back, they'd be so relieved to see me that they'd forget about how raging they were. I wondered if Mum had been ringing, and if so, what the heck they were all going to tell her. But I couldn't let myself get too distracted. When you're studying your own ancestors' childhood and taking as many notes as I was trying to—well, it's a full-time job. You have to stay focused. You can only take care of one time zone at a time. That's something I've definitely learned. It's a useful thing that everyone should know.

So when Kevin said, "Well? You ready?" I said I was. A hundred percent.

The animals snorted and whinnied at us. Kevin patted them and said, "Easy, girl. Easy, fella," and then we all went out of the courtyard and those horses were excellent, all serene and obedient. John would have gone mental if anyone had tried to attach him to a cart like that.

Ghostly fingers of fog had started to drift around the trees again. Kevin had brought a blanket, and the two of us climbed up onto the cart, and he said, "Go on, go on," and Ross and Somerville started trotting along, as if being hooked up to a cart with two nearly full-size humans on it was perfectly grand. Kevin spread the rug over our knees, like we were old people.

There was nothing old about the way we took off. We picked up a load of speed, down a new and different driveway. This was the way to the north gates, he said.

Soon we were rattling along, tearing down to the end of that drive with this new gateway staring us in the face. I scrunched up my eyes, half ready to cross back over some time threshold or other as soon as we went out onto the road. I was on the brink of saying good-bye. But when I opened my eyes, we were already outside and the roads were made of mud. I laughed a bit. The wind was getting stronger, and I could feel the cart wobbling as gusts of it invisibly belted against us from all directions.

"Wow, I'm still here," I whispered.

And Kevin went, "Of course you are. Where else would you be?"

It turns out that it's easier to talk to someone who's on a fast-moving cart than it is in practically any other situation that exists.

"Hey, Kevin, I hope you don't think this is a personal question or anything, but how did you lose that finger?"

He looked down at his hand and he went, "Good God! My finger. It's missing!"

It must have been the first time he'd ever cracked that particular joke, because he laughed for ages, and it was kind of infectious. When we calmed down, I said, "No, but seriously, what actually did happen?"

"I'm a stable boy, aren't I? Finger loss is an occupational hazard. All it takes is one moment of daydreaming, and whack!"

He did this big exaggerated mime of a hammer banging down on his hand. "Learned a good lesson, though. There are times for daydreaming, but then there are other times when it's not such a good idea."

"Do you miss it?"

"Well, it is a bit of a nuisance when I'm trying to point at something, but apart from that I get on fairly well without it."

I told Kevin all about how my mother had left me to go and work in Australia, even though I hardly ever discussed that with anyone because nobody usually knew what to say. As far as I know, it's not that usual for someone's mother to go off to a whole other continent. He listened to me very carefully. He didn't go into bogus sympathy mode like some people do when you tell them stuff like that, and he didn't interrupt or ask me how I felt about it or how I was coping or any other useless thing at all. He waited until I'd finished, and when I had, he said it sounded like I missed her quite a lot, and I said yes I did, sometimes.

And then he told me a bit more about this girl we were going to collect, and of course the whole time I knew exactly who he was talking about. He said she was great, and he went on about how she had this dark curly hair and a face as pale as eggshell.

"Sounds as if you quite like her," I said, which was obviously the understatement of the entire century.

I asked him why hadn't he gone to get her before now, and he said he already had, but her parents had sent him away because he'd turned up on his own out of the blue on a horse, with no documentation or advance warning or anything.

"Stop me if I'm wrong," I said, "but isn't that exactly what we're doing again now?"

He grinned and said there was one crucial difference this time. And the crucial difference was me. Me and the cart.

No one ever went into service in Blackbrick, or "the big house," which is what everyone called it, without hearing formally from the owner or one of his representatives. The Blackbrick cart was always sent, not a wild local boy riding bareback on a horse. If the cart wasn't sent, then nobody could be sure the arrangement was above board. That's why the last time he'd gone to get her, they hadn't allowed her to go.

My chancer of a granddad was trying to smuggle her in. And this was his second attempt.

Then he told me that I was going to have to pretend to be the nephew of Lord Corporamore. I wished he'd let me know about that a bit sooner than three minutes before we were due to arrive.

He told me that he was going to hide behind the cart and that I was to tell them my name was Cyril, which apparently he thought was a pretty realistic name for Corporamore's nephew to have.

I didn't argue, although I'd have preferred a nonstupid name for once in my life, even if it was only for a few minutes.

Kevin handed me the reins. He said if I kept on being this good, he'd let me drive on the way back, too. The cart was rattly, and Ross's and Somerville's hooves clopped in a lovely way, making an uplifting kind of sound on the ground beneath, and the wind blew, fresh and energetic and whistly, and there was only one thing I kept thinking about.

Very soon I'd be seeing her.

It was a tiny little house in the middle of a row of other houses. I went to the door.

A load of kids stood very still, staring at me with serious faces. When I said that my name was Cyril Corporamore, I thought I saw a couple of compassionate looks, but I might have been imagining that.

I shook her parents' hands and I studied their faces while at the same time trying to act as if I had no special connection to them at all.

"Hello," I said.

They both said, "How do you do, sir?" as if I was someone important.

I said that I'd been sent by George Corporamore, even though being an imposter like that is something that can get you into quite a lot of trouble. I showed them the Blackbrick cart, which Kevin was now crouching behind, and I said that I was there to inform them that the whole plan about their daughter coming to the big house was a hundred percent genuine.

I went on to say that I was sorry about the previous mix-up when Kevin had come on his own, and that of course we should have notified them in advance and how when I thought about it—ha, ha, ha—they must have been very suspicious about the whole arrangement.

And they said they hadn't meant to be uncooperative but that Kevin's late-night arrival had seemed a little strange, and we all exchanged these friendly knowing looks with one another. I was more or less brilliant the way I lied about everything.

They asked me if I had a letter, and by then I'd had a major crash course in thinking on my feet, so I said we'd arrange to have that sent on, and they nodded their heads as if they thought that was totally grand.

Everyone in the house was rustling about and there were screeches and cries and other noises mingled together—a mixture of excitement and worry. The kids clustered around, still staring, making me feel kind of edgy.

I did it, though. I pulled it off. It was stressful because of the pressure that comes from being a massive liar. For a while I thought the thudding in my head was never going to stop. But then she came to the door and it did stop. Everything did.

I wondered why nobody had ever told me how ridiculously good-looking my gran was. I also wondered why she'd never told me about the squillion brothers and sisters she had. I must have had all these old relatives that she'd never said anything about as long as I'd known her, which is my whole life. When she was old, Granny Deedee was forever going on about how important family is, and how you need to stay close to your loved ones. So it seemed strange that she'd never said a single word about this whole gang-load of brothers and sisters and I was only finding out about them now.

Before she left her house, she held each of the children's faces and kissed them on the tops of their heads. Standing in the doorway, her dad blew his nose and her mum stroked her hair and buttoned up her thin coat. I tried to assure them that she was in safe hands and that everything was going to be fine, not that you can ever really guarantee anyone anything like that. I did my best to seem like I knew what I was talking about, but I have to admit that I found it difficult to say anything at all. It was mainly because of her face and how beautiful it was.

Kevin was still hiding behind the cart. She walked with me backward down the little scraggy path, waving at her mum and dad and all those kids. I told them that there was no need for them to keep waving us off. I told them to go inside or they'd freeze. Eventually they closed the door. And then Kevin jumped out from his hiding place, and she nearly died. When she'd recovered, he took her by the hand, all gentle and tender. As she climbed up into the cart, her messy hair brushed against my face by accident and I could feel her breath on my skin, and something inside me started to get warm.

Kevin put the blanket around her, and he kept saying, "How are you?" and she kept saying, "I'm the finest. It's so wonderful to see you."

They were obviously much too busy talking to each other to think about practical things like driving the cart, so I took the reins, and the horses started trotting back toward the Abbey.

"Kevin, I can't believe it—you came back for me, just as you promised," she said, and he went on about how he was someone who never broke his promises, as if I weren't even there and as if I hadn't had anything to do with the whole thing.

I thought then would be an excellent moment to unveil the truth. The timing was more or less perfect and I was feeling quite excited. So without waiting for another second I said, "Hey, guess what? I know a whole load of things about you." And I was feeling all knowledgeable and wise, the way only time travelers can.

"For example," I continued, looking at her, "I know what your name is." She looked at Kevin, and then they stared at me in a not-particularly-impressed way.

"Your name's Deedee."

There was a kind of spooky silence for a while, and I assumed they were absorbing my brilliance.

"Deedee?" they both said then. "Who's Deedee?"

"Don't worry," Kevin whispered to her, and he tapped his half finger on the side of his head, which I knew for a fact was his way of saying there was a lunatic on board.

They told me that neither of them had ever even heard of anyone called Deedee in their lives.

"This is Maggie," he said, pointing to her with that finger again. "Maggie McGuire."

And his voice was as certain and solid as a bullet whistling toward me.

Chapter 9

IT WAS all wrong.

This girl looked like she was about fifteen, maybe even sixteen, and she had a ton of siblings that Granny Deedee never had, as far as I knew. This girl was a different person completely.

Oh no, I said to myself. *I'm tampering with history here. I'm interfering with the natural order of things.* It wasn't until then that I realized how hazardous the whole thing was. You're not supposed to mess with the past like that.

The point is that if you want to exist, then your grandfather has to marry a very specific person, and in my case that person's name was not Maggie McGuire. And now there was a massive question mark over me and my whole basic future existence.

So I went, "Whoa!" and I pulled the reins, and the horses slowed down and then they came to a total stop.

"Cosmo, what are you doing?" Kevin said. "Keep going! We've got to get back as quickly as we can. This is no time to relax."

"I'm not relaxed," I said, which was definitely true.

"Excuse me for a second," I said to Maggie then, and she looked at me and smiled.

It's very hard to explain what it was like to have Maggie smile at you, even under stressful conditions like the ones I was in. I could supply you with a load of details, like for example that her hair was all messy and her face was all pale and oval and everything, but that still doesn't really give you an idea.

So anyway, I asked Kevin if he wouldn't mind stepping off the cart for a moment, there was something I needed to discuss with him in private, and it was important.

"What the bloody hell, in the name of all that's holy, are you doing?" he asked after we'd both jumped down onto the muddy ground.

"There's something I really need to discuss with you. Something to do with you and this girl. You see, the thing is, she's not who she's supposed to be at all."

"God almighty," he whispered, his voice kind of gravelly and grim. "You need to keep out of this. This is none of your business."

He was only a young boy himself, way too young to be thinking about making a lifelong commitment to some-body, especially someone who he wasn't supposed to end up with anyway.

The other quite big problem was that she was gorgeous. And if he did end up with her like he said he was going to, then I was pretty sure it meant he wouldn't be ending up with Granny Deedee, and if he didn't do that, then I'd basically never be born.

Typical me to get tied up in a situation like this.

"I want you to know, for your information, that you can't marry her."

And he went, "Why not?" and I went, "Well, for one thing, you're only a kid," and he said, "No, I'm not. I'm sixteen, and that's a very good age for people to start thinking about their future."

I told him that as far as I was concerned, thinking about the future was fantastically overrated.

"Look, how many girls have you actually met in your life?"

He admitted that he hadn't met very many, and I said, "See? See? How can you possibly know that she's the one if you haven't had a proper look around? There might be billions of other girls in a whole load of other places who could be perfect for you."

And it was around then that I realized that even if your life is rubbish, the idea of not being born . . . Well, let's just say I didn't think it was a particularly good option.

"Okay, anyway, listen," I said. "I've changed my mind, and the thing is that we can't bring her to Blackbrick. We need to take her back to her house. Because I know for a fact that she's *not* your future. Everything's going to get screwed up if you marry her, and I'm not going to let that happen."

I stood facing him, trying to make myself into somebody that he wasn't going to argue with. But it didn't work. He had this big, annoyed look on his face.

"Right. Hold on a moment now. Who are you to be telling me my business? What suddenly makes you such a know-it-all about the things that I should and shouldn't do and about decisions that have got nothing to do with you? Get back up into the cart and get moving," he growled. He was pointing ahead and acting like I was his personal slave.

"No, I won't," I said.

"Well, grand," he said, "because it doesn't make any difference to me. I'll be just as happy to leave you here."

"Well, if you do that, then I'll go back and tell her parents the truth. I'll tell them, Lord Corporamore doesn't know anything about this whole creepy, dodgy arrangement."

I definitely wasn't ready for what he did next.

He snatched my shirt and started to swing me around. I tried not to let him, but it turns out he was very strong. Then he dragged me onto the ground.

He curled his hand into a knobbly fist and he punched me in the face, and I could feel a dead prickly burn, which was the beginning of a massive purple swelling that ended up staying on my face for a good while afterward.

I was lying on the ground then, and he had his foot on my chest and was pointing his toe at my chin, and he was going on about how his will was greater than mine.

"Why are you threatening to scupper me? I'm the one

who let you stay. I should have told you to go back to wher-ever you bloody well came from as soon as I first saw you. And you know I can still get rid of you now. All I have to do is tell Corporamore you're here, scribbling things down in that notebook and not having any proof of identity and suchlike."

I spoke to him as clearly as I was able to, even though by then I felt extremely dizzy.

"Listen to me for a second, Kevin. Will you please listen? I know things that you don't know and I'm from a place that none of you has been, and I need you to trust me. Maggie's not supposed to be your destiny and you're not supposed to be hers, and if you do become each other's destinies, then a load of people will be in trouble, including me."

"What kind of trouble are you talking about?" he asked, all out of breath.

"Nonexistence trouble. My life is probably hanging in the balance as we speak."

He looked at me as if I was the saddest person he'd met in his entire life.

"It's hard to explain. And I know it sounds weird and everything. But I need you to believe me. Please."

My voice got smaller and smaller. Suddenly I felt kind of humiliated. I think it was because of the way he was look-ing at me, and how extremely weird he obviously thought I was. I could feel myself sort of slumping down as if the air had been let out of me. I was scared that I was in the middle of wiping out my own future, but as well as that, I was disappointed. If you've been all geared up to meet the young version of your gran and then you realize that in fact you've collected someone who isn't actually her, that's disappointing in its own strange way.

"And all *I* need *you* to do is listen carefully to *me*. Because this is the last time I'm telling you: Maggie McGuire is coming with us to Blackbrick. Nothing's going to stop that from happening. Do you understand? If you're still planning to thwart me, then I will do you another injury, and this time you might never recover from it. But I don't think you really want to thwart me, do you?"

If I'd known what "thwart" actually meant, I might have been in a better position to comment.

He took his foot off my chest, and I sat up.

By then Maggie had climbed off the cart.

"Kevin? God almighty. What in heaven's name are you doing to Lord Corporamore's poor nephew?"

They stood quite close to me, but for a while I couldn't get up off the ground. I grabbed clumps of mud out of the earth and kind of threw them so they scattered off in a load of different directions.

After that he didn't say another single mean thing to me. He waited for a bit until I calmed down.

"All right, easy there," he said. "You are being a terrible nuisance, but all the same I don't like to see anyone so grieved."

I felt like telling him if he didn't like it, he shouldn't have given me that punch in the head.

"Kevin, what's happened to you? What on earth . . . ? This boy doesn't wish us any ill. He's helping us. Aren't you, Cyril?" She looked at me and smiled one of her fantastic smiles.

I wondered if he really did feel bad, or whether he was just trying to impress his girlfriend.

"I didn't mean to be so rough with you," he said quite softly then. "But you see, I'm not letting anyone come between me and Maggie, and the fellow who threatens to do that will make me furious. That's my position on the matter. I'm not apologizing for it, though I do admit to having gotten a bit carried away there. Now I'm going to ask you this one question, and the question is: Are you still going to help us?"

I rolled over on the cold ground and I pushed myself up onto my feet and staggered around for a bit.

I know it's a pretty unlikely thing to happen, but in case you ever meet your granddad when he's young, don't be too aggressive to him, not even if you've been provoked.

"Okay, okay. I'll still help," I said, even though something inside my brain felt like it was sinking into the quicksand of time.

So then we were up on the cart again, and Maggie laughed a little bit and said, "Well, goodness me. I'm very glad we got that sorted out."

And that's how Kevin's plan to bring her to Blackbrick was suddenly back in the middle of happening, and the horses were trotting up the north avenue, and I knew then that if I was going to have any chance of existing in the future, I was going to have to figure out a plan of my own, and I was going to have to do it quite soon.

By then my young granddad didn't seem to care about anything apart from her. They kept looking at each other without blinking, until eventually I had to say, "Guys, delighted you're so happy to see each other and everything, but would you mind waiting until we get back to the stables for this, because I'm the one who has to steer the cart, and I kind of need to be able to concentrate."

It was obvious that both of them were totally on the love train. And the problem is that love like that can be a very difficult thing to reverse.

Chapter 10

IT'S NOT like I didn't know how bizarre the whole thing was—meeting my granddad when he was a kid, and then meeting this lovely strange girl who wasn't my grandmother but whom he worshipped, and helping to get the two of them together—and realizing that if I actually wanted a chance of existing, then getting him together with someone who wasn't my gran was not in my best interests, to put it mildly. It sounds completely mad, I know, and I wouldn't have believed it myself—that's if it hadn't happened. There might be people who could reckon that I was having one massive big hallucination because maybe I was mad myself. But just because you can't explain something scientifically doesn't mean it's been invented by the murky recesses of your own sad little brain. Weird things happen. That's the thing about being alive: it's totally weird.

I had no idea what the plan was when we got back, but it turns out that Kevin had a good few of the practicalities already taken care of. He'd been organizing them for ages, apparently.

There was this whole big bit of Blackbrick that nobody ever went to anymore. It was called Crispin's wing, and it's where we took Maggie. She had started to get suspicious—obviously, because she wasn't stupid—asking why were we creeping around like that, but Kevin kept telling her to trust him, and she kept saying *of course* she trusted him, and he said, "No more questions, then—not until we get everything settled."

We walked along a brown shiny corridor. To the right at the end of it, there was a thick door scarred with deep cracks, like old wounds. Kevin pushed it open. On the other side was a cold room, very dusty, with wind coming in gushes down a big stained fireplace. There were brushes and cloths and a bucket stacked in the grate. It looked as if someone had once been in the middle of cleaning it but had given up for some sudden reason. Kevin weaved across the room, past saggy armchairs and sofa-shaped objects, which were all covered in blotchy gray sheets. There was another door, and behind it was a much comfier type of a place, with a wide, clean bed and warm-looking blankets. A proper fire must have been lit earlier in the day. It was dying down now but was still smoldering in its grate, and breathing out little occasional glows of brightness. A fat candle glimmered on a low table. There was a huge book-shelf that went up to the ceiling. All of the shelves dipped in gentle curves, weighed down by heavy hardbacks. There was a mirror and a comfortable-looking chair. I thought about my own small, cold room and my flat mattress for a jealous second or two.

She kept saying how perfectly lovely it all was and that she felt like a queen and how comfortable the bed looked, and I said, "Yeah, it totally does."

"Will you be all right here for a while?" Kevin asked. And she said, "Oh, indeed I will." Then he said we had to go, or else Mrs. Kelly'd be wondering where we were. As we moved toward the door, he held out his hand to me and we did a handshake.

"Thanks, Cosmo."

"Cosmo?" said Maggie from the bed. "I thought his name was Cyril."

Kevin told her to get some sleep and that very soon he'd explain everything properly. We had to leave her there and get back to the main part of the Abbey.

"I really am grateful to you for helping us the way you did. I couldn't have done it without you," said Kevin. And even though I knew there was a serious risk that I'd more or less secured my own future annihilation that night, still there was a part of me that felt quite good.

Chapter 11

IT TURNS OUT that the place where we put Maggie was where Cordelia's brother once used to live, except that he didn't live there anymore. He didn't live anywhere. He was dead. He'd died on a break from being a soldier. There at Blackbrick. To me it sounded like freakishly bad luck, someone dying when they were on *holiday* from the war.

Kevin told me that ever since then, George Corporamore had been a different man. All angry and restless and often loitering around the place in the middle of the night, or wandering down to the stables early in the morning before the sun came up, whispering his son's name and generally behaving like a bit of a loolah.

I didn't ask for any details because it wasn't any of my business, but Kevin told me a few things about Crispin too: that his parents had loved him very much, which I'm sure was true; that he had been a pretty courageous guy; and that he had been by far the most popular Corporamore at the Abbey for generations. From what I could make out, he'd helped a load of people to escape from some terrible battle in the middle of the war, even though their faces and arms had been blown off and even though it has been quite difficult for him because he'd had something inside him called "shrapnel" and also because he'd been in a permanent state of horror.

Crispin had been a hero, which just goes to prove that having a weird name doesn't necessarily predict how you're going to behave in a crisis.

Later that night I was feeling a bit on my own, so I went off to Crispin's wing myself, and Kevin was there, sitting on Maggie's bed. Maggie said hello and Kevin smiled. It made me feel really good the way they both seemed happy to see me.

Pretty soon we were chatting among the three of us. She asked us when she was expected to start work and what her jobs were going to be.

"Maggie, just to let you know, you don't really have a job here," I explained helpfully, and I also confirmed that my name was not Cyril and that I wasn't a Corporamore.

"Oh, Kevin, you haven't!" she said, turning to him again. I couldn't tell whether she looked happy or sad.

"Haven't what?" he asked. I couldn't tell whether he looked guilty or proud.

"You have. I knew it. You've SMUGGLED me in here. Oh, for the love of God."

"Well figured out," I said a bit sarcastically. But Kevin was very good at soothing a person when a person had just realized that something dodgy was going on. He told her for around the fifteenth time that she was to trust him. He'd work on everything and it was all going to be grand. Eventually she didn't even seem that annoyed or worried that she'd been brought there under false pretenses. In fact she seemed a little bit thrilled, as if it made everything even better than she'd thought—as if as far as she was concerned it made Kevin even more fabulous than ever.

He kept saying he was on top of it, and that all he had to do was have a few conversations with some people at Blackbrick and she wouldn't have to be kept a secret anymore. But I knew he was thinking on his feet. He hadn't a clue how things were going to work out with Maggie. He didn't know how anything was going to work out. Nobody does.

I'd forgotten to tell Kevin about how Maggie's parents had asked for a letter, so I filled him in. And when I did, Kevin was all, "Can you write it for me?"

"Why don't you do it yourself?" I asked him.

"I can't," he said.

"Why not?"

"Because I haven't got around to learning."

He told me to stop looking so shocked. He reminded me that I hadn't known how to hitch a horse to a cart. He said that he'd had quite a busy childhood in which he had learned to do lots of useful things, but writing didn't happen to be one of them. And neither was reading.

"You can't *read*?"

Maggie said that neither could she. She didn't sound as if

she thought it was anything to be particularly embarrassed about.

It's amazing the things you can find out if you go to the past; for example, you might learn that your own grand-father was illiterate when he was already sixteen years old. If either he or Maggie had been in my year, they'd have been made to go to remedial after-school with D. J. Burke and the Geraghty twins. It was disturbing, this information about their very bad education, and I wasn't too eager to dwell on it. I had enough on my plate already.

But I did tell them that while I was here, I might be able to give them a few quick tips on how to read and write, and Kevin said, "Do if you like," but he didn't sound that enthu-siastic or appreciative about it or anything.

I went to see Maggie on my own the next morning before anyone else was up. I told her I was sorry for calling so early, but she said it was fine. She'd been awake anyway.

And I said, "You must be starting to be sorry that Kevin picked you up, seeing as you don't really have a job here or anything."

"I'm not sorry at all. To be honest with you, I consider it the most wonderful thing anyone could ever have done for me. I've been wishing for this for I can't tell you how long."

"Don't you find it a tiny bit disturbing? Aren't you wor-ried about it?" I asked her.

"Worried about what?" she said, her massive brown eyes

shining at me all round and big and, well, you know . . . lovely.

"About what those Corporamore owners would do if they found you here? About being in a massive amount of trouble for trespassing and illegal entry, and for being a stowaway?"

She said that it was pretty much impossible to be scared or worried now that she was with Kevin. She was still talking about him like he was the most fabulous guy on the entire planet, and I think I already knew that nothing I said was going to make any difference. But I didn't give up for ages. I tried to explain to her all about what a lousy place this was to work. I told her about Cordelia and her brattishness, and how Kevin spent more or less every morning trying to make a perfect breakfast for her but it was never good enough, and how he always had to apologize to her for basically nothing. I kept on saying, "Really, Maggie, it might seem like a superb place to be, but to be honest with you, working here is lousy."

All the more reason for her to stay, she explained. To be company for Kevin and me, and to keep our spirits up.

"You're wrong, Maggie. You're much better off cutting your losses and going home again. I'm not hanging around here for too long myself. I have a home to go back to. I'll be gone by the end of the week, and if you have any sense, you will be too."

She wasn't listening to me. I don't think she would have listened to anyone except Kevin.

I asked her about all her little brothers and sisters, and I said they must be missing her a lot and maybe some of them were crying, wishing for her to come back, and wouldn't they be so thrilled if she did. It was below the belt, I know, but when you're desperate, you have to use whatever tactics happen to be available at the time.

She said that she did miss her family, and she admitted that it had been heartbreaking to say good-bye, and her eyes got a bit misty. For a second I thought I had her, but then she swiftly went on to say that Kevin was her savior, blah blah blah, and she didn't want to be anywhere that he wasn't, blah blah blah . . . and what a prince of a guy he was.

I only had a couple more days before I had to get back home and give Granddad lessons about the past so that he'd pass the memory test and nobody would take him away. It wasn't a heck of a lot of time. But it's a big job, trying to split people up who were never meant to be together. Plus, neither of them was making it very easy for me.

A little later the same morning, for example, Kevin had legged it off to Crispin's wing to be with Maggie before I even got to the kitchen. Mrs. Kelly was there smoothing down her apron, and when I arrived, she straightened my hair a bit like she was a gran and not a strange woman in an old house, and she said, "Now, Cosmo, Kevin was supposed to be doing all manner of duties today, but he is busy and he's said you'll do them instead. And of course, it's irregular to have visitors working for their keep, but times have changed, as we keep telling you, and I daresay it might do you a world of good."

"Yeah, I daresay that as well," I said, and the whole time I was thinking that I knew exactly what Kevin was "busy" with. Busy trying to snog Maggie in Crispin's wing, that's what. Anyway, the point was that I definitely couldn't leave those two alone together for very long. It wasn't safe. I could picture him going on about exactly how much he fancied her the whole time, and then asking her to marry him, and I already knew that it wouldn't take too much persuasion before she said yes.

I was about to tell Mrs. Kelly that I had no time to do anyone's chores, least of all Kevin's. I was on the verge of heading off to Crispin's wing myself with the intention of being a tactical third wheel, when something crept across my brain. It was an idea, and the idea was that I was going to rat out my own granddad.

Chapter 12

IT'S QUITE interesting how someone can go from being a loyal, trustworthy grandson to being king of the rats in a relatively short space of time. All it takes is a few changes in your life circumstances.

I asked Mrs. Kelly what duties I was supposed to do, and she started reeling off a whole massive list of things, and I wrote them all down in my notebook because there were too many to remember. And she was impressed because I was able to write, and she asked me where I was from and who my family were, even though she'd promised she wasn't going to ask me stuff like that. I told her I wasn't able to talk about my past, it was too painful, which is a great way to stop people from asking nosy questions that you're not too interested in answering.

The first thing on the list of duties was to make Cordelia's breakfast and take it up to her. I could feel my plan firming up. After that I was to clear out the grates of three fires, sweep the kitchen floor, peel a massive bucket of potatoes, polish the furniture in the hall, and feed the horses. I told Mrs. Kelly she could count on me, no problem, and she said, "Lord above, Cosmo, but you really are a great fellow altogether," and I said, "Thanks." Being called a great fellow was a few notches up from being called madder than a brush. It felt like I was making progress.

She looked at me a bit dreamily as I started getting Cordelia's breakfast ready. She said my name a few times, and then she asked how on earth I'd come to be called something so unusual. I told her that I wished I knew.

I'd figured out exactly what I was going to do by then, and it was lousy, but at the time I didn't think I had much of an option.

When I knocked on Cordelia's door, she was just as rude to me as she'd been to Kevin.

"Oh, come IN," she said. And when I did go in, her face was hard and sharp, her words bitter and cross. She asked me who the devil I was, and I told her I was a new person come to help for a few days.

"I didn't give anyone permission to send a strange new boy to me. Where's Kevin?"

I told her that Kevin was busy. I told her that I was a family friend of Mrs. Kelly's and that I was above board in every way. But I said there was something else going on that was completely below board and she might want to know about it. Cordelia started nibbling on the corner of one of the pieces of crustless toast, and she looked into my eyes and said, "Very well, then. What is it?"

"There's this girl who's been smuggled in here, and now

she's sleeping over and she's planning to stay. I don't think your dad would be that thrilled if he found out about it."

"A girl?" Cordelia said, pensively pouring herself some tea, steam rising in front of her face.

"Yes, a girl."

"Who smuggled her in?" she said, *plink*ing two sugar cubes into her cup and making a little tea whirlpool with the skinny silver spoon.

"Look, all I'm going to say is that at the moment she's asleep in the old wing where your brother used to live."

She stopped stirring, put the spoon back down on the tray, and blinked a few times.

"Did you know my brother?" she said, and her arrogant little voice changed for a moment.

"No. I didn't. But anyway, that's where she is."

"Father doesn't allow anyone to go in there, not even me. If he finds out there's a strange girl staying there without anyone's consent, he is going to lose his sense of reason."

Excellent, I thought.

"Don't you think you'd better tell him, then?"

"Yes," she said, staring out the window, munching away. "Yes, I very much think I ought to. Father and I shall be dining together this evening, and I shall use that as an opportunity to inform him of the situation."

"Great," I said.

"By the way, how is it that *you* know about this girl?"

I told her that I'd prefer not to get into the details, just that I knew a lot of stuff that other people didn't know, and that was all I was prepared to say. I also told her not to tell her father who she had gotten the information from. I sold the idea to her by saying that if she didn't reveal her sources, she'd get all the credit herself.

Her eyes went kind of flickery and gray for a second like she was suspicious, and as if she thought I was some kind of snake or weasel. And I suppose if you want to be precise about it, that's what I was, but I was acting for a good cause, even though it might have seemed mean at the time.

After filling Cordelia in on Maggie, I had to go and do all of Kevin's other jobs. And I kept on thinking how much I hoped my plan to get Maggie kicked out was going to work.

I thought I had the whole thing in order: Corporamore was going to find out about Maggie and go mad and send her away, and she would go back to where she'd come from, where she had all those brothers and sisters who loved her so much, and Kevin would be able to get on with the life that he was meant to have, not the one he thought he wanted, and I'd go back home to the present, and that would basically be that.

"The best way to make the gods laugh is to tell them your plans," is what my granddad used to say. I'm sure if I'd listened that day for a second, I would have heard a thousand gods laughing their heads off.

❧   ❧   ❧

By the middle of the morning, I was already a hundred percent wrecked, partly because of the stress but mainly because of all the heavy lifting and slave labor. I legged it down to the kitchen, where I bumped straight into Kevin, who apparently was "nipping up" to get himself and Maggie a cup of tea. Very *Romeo and Juliet*. I had a disturbing image of the two of them sitting at the end of Crispin's bed, sipping from the polite little china cups, both of them saying, "Ah, fantastic" together.

He asked me how I was getting on with the work, and I said fine but that to be perfectly honest, I didn't have much time to hang out and chat because I still had a ton more of it to do.

And he said, "You've no idea how wonderful it has been to spend time with her," and I said, "No, I'm sure I haven't a clue."

In my head I was thinking that pretty soon Cordelia would have briefed her father and Kevin and Maggie would be ratted out and everything would be okay.

Mrs. Kelly made dinner for the Corporamores and hobbled up with it to the dining room herself. She reported that by the time she was serving pudding, Lord George Corporamore had drunk a whole bottle of brandy. You can't always predict when people are going to do things like that. And you definitely can't predict the way they're going to behave after they've done it.

I sprinted off to Crispin's wing. Maggie was asleep, like an angel in a white nightshirt with her messy black hair all spread out over the pillow and the pale skin of her cheek looking kind of like it was glowing.

I made it in just ahead of him and hid under the bed. And then almost instantly I heard the *thud*s and *bang*s of George Corporamore's feet getting closer and closer, and I could hear him bursting in through the doorway and I was realizing that this whole thing was my responsibility now, and if something bad happened to her, it would be because of me.

From where I was hiding, I could see his boots in the doorway, and they were very pointy. And I could feel the bed creaking, which must have been Maggie waking up.

"Who the blazes are you? What are you doing in this bed? NO ONE is ALLOWED in here. Do you hear me? This is a place where people are FORBIDDEN. Explain yourself immediately," he demanded, and I was thinking this was all going to go horribly wrong now.

More rustling, and I imagined her eyes opening, and I was thinking about her face.

"Hello, sir. My name is Maggie. Maggie McGuire."

She always cast a spell on people—at least that's what I think always used to happen. Soon I could hear his voice softening and sounding a hundred percent gentler. He went on then about how there once was a person who used to sleep in this bed and who had curly hair too. And at first I wasn't sure what the sound was, but I realized that what I was hearing was George Corporamore starting to cry.

"Forgive me," I could hear him say. "He was my son. I once had a son. His name was Crispin."

And then, right in front of my face, Corporamore's knees hit the ground, which looked as if it could have been quite painful, and there were all these sniffling, sobby kinds of noises, and a few minutes went by, and Maggie said, "I'm so sorry, sir." He sobbed away at the end of the bed. And she said, "Hush, hush. There, there," the way you might talk to a baby.

Maggie had obviously had a load of practice comforting people when they were crying. She was very good at it. Corporamore stopped sobbing and quietened down altogether. He said to her how wrong it had felt for this room to have become so empty and cold, and how now that it was warm again and had some life in it, it reminded him of the way things used to be. He went on about how warmth brings memories alive and how coldness keeps them dead.

I got kind of paralyzed for a bit, but eventually I slid out from under the bed, which was risky. And before I managed to sneak away, I stood there for a second, feeling like a big idiot. They didn't see me, but still for some reason I was mortified.

Chapter 13

KEVIN WAS still very happy for me to be on Cordelia Corporamore's breakfast duty for the few days I was going to be here. And I was happy about it too—I didn't want him talking to her and finding out that I was a miserable informer and that I had spilled the beans about Maggie and that because of me, Cordelia had gone and told her father.

In fact, it turned out that her father wanted a word with me and Kevin. I walked into the kitchen to find Mrs. Kelly telling Kevin that George Corporamore wanted to see us in connection with the smuggling of a girl onto the premises.

"God almighty, Kevin, but the same question occurs to me for the second time in as many days: Why didn't you come to me? It's pure silly of you lads to have done this without at least explaining to me what you were planning. If you needed help, then you should have come straight to me. Isn't that the way it used to be, Kevin?"

"I know. I didn't want to get anyone in trouble," Kevin said, deliberately making his eyes wide and innocent-looking.

And Mrs. Kelly said, "Well, all I can say is that you're terrible altogether. And when you get back from talking to Lord

Corporamore, you're to fill me in on what has happened and who this girl is, and honestly, don't you know that you can be assured that I can help? Do you not know me by now, Kevin? Lord George is waiting for you in his study, so now it would be in both your interests to get yourselves up there as quickly as possible and explain yourselves to him. Mind your manners and prepare for an act of contrition, do you hear me? He'll be raging with the pair of you."

We left the kitchen with Kevin spitting out words under his breath. "It must have been Cordelia. How did that brat find out? I'm going to kill her." I started to get hot, the way you do when you're filling up with shame. I started to imagine what Kevin might do if he found out it was me who was the rat.

He told me there were sixty-four steps from the kitchen to Corporamore's study, even though at the time I wasn't really in the mood for Blackbrick trivia. I was too busy feeling very uneasy about what was waiting for us at the top.

He said, "Leave the talking to me," which was absolutely fine as far as I was concerned.

When we got there and knocked on the door, a voice from inside said, "Come," and we walked in.

It was the first time I got a proper look at his face. George Corporamore was sitting behind a big varnished desk. There were red curtains, shimmering in the light of a crackling, spitting fire. He was holding a massive cigar between his fingers, and he was looking the two of us up and down.

It was then that it began to occur to me the extent of the serious trouble we might both be in.

He was more or less the pointiest man I had ever seen in my life. His chin was pointy. His nose was pointy. His ears. His clothes. His shoes. His fingers. Even his eyes were like little pins, piercing and poking at us from his triangular face.

He didn't look like the kind of man who would kneel and cry at the end of someone's bed.

He asked me to introduce myself. He said that Mrs. Kelly had told him about how she had hired me in a temporary capacity because of what a great horseman I was, which was news to me. He wanted us to tell him whether we had been responsible for bringing a young girl into the Abbey, and for putting her in his son's room. A place where nobody had been permitted to go for more than two years now.

Kevin's hands were in his pockets and he was standing with his legs wide apart. If you hadn't been as close up to him as I was, you'd probably never have seen the small blob of sweat sliding down the side of his face. And you definitely wouldn't have thought he was the tiniest bit scared.

He went on about what a great worker Maggie was and how he was dead familiar with her family and what decent people they were. And he said that it was not the slightest bit "apt" for boys to be bringing breakfast to Miss Cordelia and that it would be very useful to have Maggie, who was happy to stay and work in exchange for room and board, and she had the appetite of a small bird, so she wouldn't be that much of a drag on the household's resources.

He definitely had a talent for talking, all right. He was a high-performance persuader, no doubt about it. At the time I reckoned that this skill was probably more useful to both of us than some of the educational things he'd missed out on, on account of being so busy learning how to take proper care of horses.

Corporamore rolled his cigar between his fingers and sucked on it from time to time so that the end of it got dark and soggy. He listened, staring at Kevin and glancing at me, until Kevin stopped talking.

He spoke in a leisurely way, like someone who'd never been in a hurry in his life. The sound of his voice made my whole body feel cold.

"I was prepared to overlook the irregularity of this boy's arrival," he said, pointing at me like I was a thing, not a person.

"And in any case, as I understand it, he'll be gone by Sunday. Furthermore, Mrs. Kelly had a part in bringing him here, which bestows upon his visit the legitimacy it requires. But now, Kevin, I'm beginning to suspect that you've lost the run of yourself altogether. What you've done is wrong. It's very wrong indeed. It makes me think that you've gotten much too big for your boots. Taking it upon yourself to smuggle a young girl into my home, my estate, my territory without my knowledge and moving her into my deceased son's quarters? I consider that most disloyal and deceitful, and by rights you should be punished very severely."

Kevin was doing his best to stay upright and non-intimidated-looking. Neither of us had a clue what Corporamore was going to say next, and after he said it, we were both very surprised that he had.

"But," Corporamore continued, "you see, now that I have met your stowaway, and now that I have a sense of what kind of a girl she is . . . well, I think that given her personableness, and her clearly burgeoning health, we can certainly make room for her here at Blackbrick, and after all, Mrs. Kelly has been needing additional help for some time. Of course, you're both extremely fortunate that I have decided on this course of action. It lets you off the hook, so to speak, but do not operate under any misconception. What I am saying to you is not an invitation for you to open the doors of Blackbrick to every vagabond you happen to think deserves some shelter. Maggie McGuire, however, is no vagabond. She is welcome to stay."

"Grand so," said Kevin, breathing out for what seemed like the first time since we'd entered the room, and I went, "Yeah, great." I made an effort to smile too, even though I totally did not feel like it.

"I'll talk to Mrs. Kelly about moving her out of Crispin's wing," added Kevin, but Lord Corporamore leaned forward on his sharp elbows and said, "No. No, she can stay there. It will be useful to have someone to warm up that part of the house, after all.

"The two of you can show her the ropes and get her organized. Now you may go."

He flicked his pointy hand toward the door, and a gold ring on his little finger flashed. Long yellow flames licked at the inside of the fireplace.

We backed out of the study. All the way down the stairs, Kevin muttered things like "What's he up to?" and "I don't trust that man at all."

But at the time, I thought that Corporamore was okay, that he had been fairly decent even though he was all pointy and had a horrible voice. I didn't know the real reason he wanted Maggie to stay. I hadn't a clue what he was planning for her. I just took him at face value.

Under the circumstances, it might have been easy to forget that I had to go home, but as the week went on, I knew I had to get back to the Granddad of my own time zone. It was getting urgent. Dr. Sally was probably already sharpening her pencils and freshening up her clipboard for her next visit. I had to be there to help Granddad review for his memory test. And now I had all these details about his life that I could fill him in on, so no one would take him away.

Pretty soon I only had one more night left at Blackbrick.

That was the night that I found out what George Corporamore really wanted from Maggie, and why he had decided
to let her stay at Blackbrick and how, the first time he'd
met her in Crispin's wing, he had interpreted her decent-
ness in the wrong way. And the only reason I found out
was because I'd forgotten a bucket and cloth near Corporamore's study, and Kevin would need it in the morning,
and so, quite late, after I'd packed my stuff back into Ted's
bag and checked for the millionth time that the key to the
south gates was in my pocket, I went up to get the equip-
ment. I was coming back down the stairs and through the
main hallway, and that was when I saw Corporamore and
Maggie standing together, very close, near the front door.

I stopped in time and hung back in the shadow of the
doorway. I knew they couldn't see me. But I could see them.
I was right there staring straight at them both.

Something happened then that I really don't ever like to
think about, even though I still sometimes do.

Corporamore's pointy-fingered hand latched on to
Maggie's shoulder. It was dark but still I could see. And then
he traced his finger along her neck and he just kept staring
at her the whole time with this horrible creepy smile on his
face.

Maggie didn't move at all. And she didn't make a sound.

He had a cigar in his other hand, and there was a glass
of brandy sitting on a silver tray. The air was thick and
blue and strong, and I thought for a terrible second that I

was going to cough. I kept on watching. I kept on wishing I could look away. But I couldn't.

And then afterward he stubbed out the cigar on the tray and he picked up the brandy glass and he walked away from her. She tucked a few strands of hair behind her ear, straightened her apron, stood very tall, and walked off in the opposite direction, her boots clicking on the wooden floor and her legs looking as if they were trembling slightly. I might have been wrong, but just then she seemed to wobble and her knees buckled as if she was about to fall.

I know there are some people who might say that this was just what I needed and I probably should have been happy. If Corporamore was doing things like that, then the romantic scenario with Maggie and Kevin was obviously on the rocks. But really it was a horrible result. He was ancient and pointy, and I knew she couldn't really like him, not in *that* way.

I didn't want anyone doing what I'd seen him do to her.

There are lots of things I wish I had done that night. But there's nothing I can do about any of it now. I wish I had chased after Corporamore and I wish I had pushed him so that his glass of brandy fell out of his hand and tumbled and shattered on the floor. I'd have been delighted if the brandy had spilled all over him. I wish he had been so shocked and astonished that he'd have dropped his big fat cigar. I like to think of it falling from his pointy, jagged, startled, pink hands and burning a massive hole in his trousers.

I wish then that I had grabbed George Corporamore and shoved him up against the wall, and I wish I'd said, "Stay away from her. Don't put your disgusting fingers anywhere near her ever again, or I'll kill you myself with my own bare hands. I swear to God I'll kill you."

There are times when I think that I did do and say all those things. I can actually see the wet stains on his clothes and the surprised look on his face, and I can see myself strong and angry and I can see Corporamore snorting and struggling with me, and I can see me holding him against the wall.

For some reason another thing I wanted to do was take Maggie by the hand. I wanted to run down to the stables with her and jump onto the horses and gallop out of Blackbrick and away. Away from this place where someone thought it was okay to do that and where she thought she had to let him.

I can see us together going really fast. I can see us laughing. It's a bit weird how I can see it quite clearly in my head even though none of it happened.

I didn't know why I wanted to protect her and save her. It was not a rational thing, but it was very powerful and it was very deep. And it never goes away.

I kept thinking then how screwed up everything was. And how it was my fault. And so I was glad that the time had come for me to go.

I stayed in the shadows, staring at the space where I'd seen Corporamore and Maggie, long after both of them had gone and the space was empty except for a twist of cigar smoke that slunk across the hall, poisoning the air.

Chapter 14

I SHOULD have left it alone. But I guess there are some things that you have to say to people even if it doesn't seem like it has anything to do with you.

When I got to Crispin's wing, I knocked. Maggie came, blurry-eyed, to the door, and I told her I was sorry if I'd woken her. She held the candle up, and her beautiful face looked a bit scary. I told her it had been great to meet her, and how sorry I was to have to say good-bye, and she said, "Why, where are you going?" as if I had nothing else to do in my life but hang around Blackbrick seeing things I didn't want to see.

I told her that I had to get out of there. She looked so calm and normal, and it was hard to believe that she'd even been in the situation I'd seen her in only a little earlier on.

"Listen, Maggie, I have a question to ask you before I go."

"What is it?" she said.

"What's the story?"

"What do you mean?" she asked.

"What I mean is that I thought you said Kevin was your destiny, but you're hardly inside the door of this place and you're letting Lord Slimeball get very familiar, if you ask me."

Her face darkened then. She walked back to Crispin's bed, and she sat down, and her eyes stayed looking at my face, but not in a good way.

"God almighty, Cosmo, what have you seen? What do you know? Why are you saying this to me?"

When people ask a load of questions all at the same time like that, it usually means they feel guilty.

"Look, I'm sorry. I don't mean to barge in on your personal business or anything."

"Well, good, because it *is* none of your business, now that you say it, and I'd be very glad if you'd put those things you've mentioned out of your head. Please, Cosmo. You need to forget."

I knew I never would, though.

We stood there looking at each other, and she was pale and lovely and I wanted to touch her face. I didn't want to squeeze her shoulder or stare darkly at her or anything creepy like that. I only wanted to put my hand on her cheek and maybe tuck some of her messy curly hair behind one of her ears or something. But I didn't. I can be kind of a coward sometimes when it comes to things like that.

"Look, Maggie, you have to do what you think is best, but you don't have to do anything that you don't want to. Don't let anyone think that you do. Okay? Kevin's not your destiny, Maggie; you're not supposed to end up with him. Don't ask me how I know that—I just do. But that guy Corporamore, he can't possibly be your destiny either."

"You don't need to worry about me. I know what I'm doing. I'm fully in charge of myself," she said.

"Well, that's good," I said to her. "Don't ever forget that."

It wasn't the greatest way to say good-bye, but it was the best I could do at the time.

I met Mrs. Kelly in the kitchen then. She was making tea. I told her I wanted to say thank you. I said it had been a great week.

"Ah yes, it has indeed," she said. "And I must say you look much better than the scrap of a lad I met a few days ago."

Kevin told me he didn't know how to thank me.

"You've done so much, Cosmo, in such a short time. And to have Maggie here, where she's safe and where we can be together, I would never have been able to do that without you. I'm very grateful."

I couldn't look him in the eye.

Kevin wasn't just my granddad anymore. Kevin was my friend. I knew it then. I know it now. I'll always know it.

I didn't tell him anything about what I'd seen Corporamore doing to Maggie. And I didn't tell him either that I'd been secretly coaching her not to fall in love with anyone. I don't blame him for wanting to marry her. I'm sure in those days every boy that ever met her probably wanted the same thing.

So I think I said, "No problem, Kevin. My pleasure."

I'd already stayed too long. The old Kevin needed me. I was going to have to leave the young Kevin to his own devices.

He asked if I wanted him to come down with me in the morning to say good-bye, and I said that would be great. I asked him to meet me at the stables. I told him there were a few important instructions I had for him. Things he needed to know about for future reference. He gave me this look, which I knew meant *Please stop being such a weirdo*. He said he'd see me in the morning. He said he was going to be sorry to say good-bye to me, and I said that I was too.

I went to my clanky little bed for the last time, and the sharp cold rain was lashing like a whip against the windows and everything was rattling. I kept wishing that I had more time. I kept wishing that I had gotten what I'd come for.

Anyone who gets to travel to the past should be able to do something really useful to make the future better, but the only thing I'd done was make people think I was a looper. I tried to comfort myself by thinking about my notebook and how it was full of handy information that was possibly going to help Granddad when I got back. But mostly I lay there looking at the bumpy ceiling. And the little window shook, and the wind screamed and whispered under the gap in the door.

Chapter 15

THERE ARE so many things I wish I had done. Big things, like killing George Corporamore. Small things, like saying a proper good-bye to Maggie. But when you're under pressure and when there are important things on your mind about someone who needs you, murdering people and saying decent good-byes aren't always too easy. And anyway, I guess there was part of me that didn't want to say good-bye at all.

I was up very early, before anyone else, which was a massive achievement. I slipped into my clothes and made my bed very carefully. I looked around my room one last time before reaching for the door.

The noises you make sound unreasonably loud when it's early in the morning and nobody else is up. My steps echoed along the flagstones. Everything in my bag jangled rowdily together as I made my way to the stables.

Nobody was there when I arrived—except, of course, for Somerville and Ross. As soon as they saw me, they thought they were going out for a run and got so excited that it made me want to cry.

"Listen, guys," I said. "Kevin will take you out later, but I have to go."

I didn't know if they understood, but they nuzzled their soft noses into my face, and I thought I wasn't going to be able to bear it. "I have to go." I said it a few more times, plunging my hand into my pocket and then pulling out the key. I could hear footsteps, louder and heavier than I ever remembered Kevin's being.

"Glad you're here. It's getting late," I said. I pressed my face into Ross's shiny neck, feeling suddenly like I wanted to stay there for a bit longer. "I'll be ready in a minute. We can go straight to the gates."

It took me a second or two to realize that it wasn't Kevin. My brain joggled as I remembered what Kevin had told me about how Lord Corporamore sometimes wandered around the stables, restless and angry, in the dark hours before dawn. And it *was* Corporamore, right there, pointy and pink, marching toward me. I held on to the key.

"What gates?" he said hissily.

"The south gates," I answered, feeling too surprised and ambushed to tell him anything except the truth.

"You must know that it is expressly forbidden for anyone, I mean anyone, to come in or go out through the south gates."

"Yes I do, but—"

"And you stand here with the audacity to tell me that you intend to defy that regulation?"

"You don't understand," I said desperately, and he agreed. I rubbed the key in my hand as if it was a magic thing that could rescue me from this uncomfortable situation. But that only made things worse, because George Corpormore suddenly fixed his little eyes on the key, and his nostrils flared with a fresh rage.

"Give. Me. That. Key. That's not your key. Tell me where you got it."

I knew then that no matter what I said, he wasn't going to believe me.

You can't see power, and you can't touch it, but it is everywhere. And the person who happens to have most of it is usually the one who thinks he's entitled to decide what happens next. His sharp hands poked at my shoulders, and he jostled me against the stable wall, shouting into my face. Bits of spit landed on my eyelids and my forehead, which was pretty disgusting. I closed my fist around the key and held it as high in the air as I could, and Corporamore kept reaching up, roughly trying to wrestle it away from me. I could hear Ross and Somerville going mental, fretting and snorting, and I knew from the sound of them that they were on my side.

"Listen to me," he grunted, as if there were some other option available to me at the time. "You weasel."

If the whole situation hadn't been so tense, I might have started to laugh.

"Relax," I said to him.

"I have no intention of relaxing until you give me back the thing that belongs to me."

And I was pinned up against the wall and his nose was approximately one millimeter from my face.

"Okay," I said. "Let go of me, will you, and I'll give it back to you. I should have given it to you ages ago, because, well, because it's yours."

He loosened his grip and then he let go completely, and I knew I was going to have to stay pretty sharp. I was shivering and my heart was hammering away like a million drums, and I could feel pints of blood galloping around in my head. But the whole time I was doing my best to be calm on the outside. I held the key out to him, and he was all confident and smug.

The sun was starting to rise, and under it the key twinkled and little bits of light shot out. And he was grinning for a second as he reached over to take it from me. I barely had time to see that smile disappear from his spiky face, because right then is when I ducked. I closed my fist tight again and I slipped past him and darted through the arch, a bit like a weasel, actually.

I ripped past the Abbey and down by the black pine trees. I scrambled along the gravel, falling to my knees a couple of times but getting up again and keeping going. The thuds of footsteps were very close behind, and someone was shouting, "Stop, Cosmo, stop." It really was Kevin this time, and because of that I did stop.

"Where were you, Kev?" I panted. "You were supposed to meet me at the stables. Why didn't you come?" A blast of unexpected wind hit my face like a slap. I could see Corporamore's shadow catching up, and there was no more time. I got up and I ran again. I ran for my life.

Running fast isn't only a sign of fear. It's also a sign of hope, which is the thing that keeps you going. I was running for my granddad and his dignity, and for the choices that I thought he still had. And for a few seconds there, I thought I was going to make it.

But then Kevin's arms clutched around my knees. He pulled me to the ground, and all the energy escaped from my body.

"Let me go! What the . . . ?"

"Cosmo, give up. You can't keep running. You've got to give him the key. You don't know what he's like. He'll pursue you forever." He went on a bit more about how this was in my best interests and how he was saving me from myself.

Corporamore was standing behind us with his hands on his hips, his mouth a tiny angry straight white line.

"Honestly, trust me, Cosmo," Kevin whispered. "It'll be better if you give it to him now. It'll save you a hell of a fight."

I lay on the cold gravel, and Corporamore strode over. "Thank you, Kevin, my boy. Glad you had the sense to put a stop to this fellow's gallop."

Corporamore pincered open my fist with his spiky hands

and plucked out the key, the way someone might pull a twisted nail from the shoe of a horse.

"I'll take that, you gurrier," he grunted.

My self-respect had disappeared by then, and quietly I started to beg. "Please, Lord Corporamore. Please. You've got to let me have it back."

"Not on your Nellie," he said, which was one of the things people used to say in those days. He smiled, threw the key up into the air, and caught it. And still I tried to change his mind. "I have to see my granddad again. I need that key. It's the only way I know to get back. I'm sorry. Please. Please . . . give it back to me."

I was pretty ashamed of the way I was acting, but I didn't know what else to do. I was embarrassed that Kevin was watching me lose all my dignity like that.

Corporamore looked at Kevin and pointed at me. "If there's one more incident involving this boy, so help me God, I'll . . . I'll . . ." He started walking back to the Abbey so that we couldn't hear what horrible thing God would help him to do if I broke the Abbey's precious rules again.

I don't know how much time went by after that, but suddenly Mrs. Kelly was there, hurrying over to the scene of my pathetic collapse, saying, "Oh, for pity's sake!"

She told us how Lord Corporamore had just been in the kitchen, ranting and calling me a young guttersnipe, talking about how I had the cheek to sneak around with keys that didn't belong to me and the nerve to do things that were forbidden. But she wasn't angry with me. Somehow I could hear in the tone of her voice that she was on my side, which felt like a tiny consolation prize in the middle of the exit strategy that had gone so wrong.

"This lad is distraught," Mrs. Kelly said to Kevin as if I weren't there at all. "This lad needs compassion and assistance. A fellow in his condition must not be hunted down like an animal just because he has a blessed key."

Kevin coaxed me into a standing position. "I'll never get back. I'll never get back now," I said under my breath. "There's someone who needs me, and I don't know if I'll ever see him again."

"There, there," said Mrs. Kelly. "Try not to be upsetting yourself." She patted me lightly on the hand, and even though that's a pretty useless thing to do, still it felt a bit nice.

"There's no going back, Cosmo. I know it's hard, but that's the way it is," Kevin said.

And Mrs. Kelly added, "You know, when you have a bit of time to think about it properly, it's just as well. Now then, I put the kettle on a little while ago, and there are some scones in the oven. I'd be very glad if you joined me for some breakfast."

I liked the sound of scones straight from the oven. And all of us reckoned we could definitely do with a cup of tea.

I went down to the horses again that night, and I think they were very glad to see I hadn't gone. I tried singing the song that my mum used to sing to me, the one that I used to whisper to John, but my voice kept cracking at the edges, so I stopped. I told them that nothing was any good, that I was stuck, but obviously they couldn't really help me. Because they were, you know, horses.

I'm sure there are people who would say I should have fought harder. Maybe I should have been a bit cleverer, a bit braver. Perhaps I should have been raging with Kevin for being the one who stopped me, but it's hard to be raging with someone who thinks he's doing his best for you, even if he has made a massive mistake. Maybe I should have stood up to George Corporamore. I sometimes think I should have tried to make things clearer to everyone. But if you weren't there at the time, it's difficult to explain.

I thought about Kevin's and Mrs. Kelly's advice about putting upsetting thoughts right out of my head and getting on with it—it seemed to be a popular theory in those days. And as a matter of fact, sometimes it's quite good advice to take.

Chapter 16

SO THAT'S more or less how I ended up staying at Blackbrick. It might be kind of hard to believe, but eventually I forgot about the present, which was pretty disloyal of me really, but partly, to be perfectly honest about it, it was also kind of great.

The trees on the driveway were as green and black and thick as ever, but the ones by the stables became bare branches as winter crept up on Blackbrick Abbey, making everything colder than the stones.

Mrs. Kelly always had a massive list of jobs for us to do, mainly cleaning and polishing. They were the kinds of jobs that took ages because of all the big rooms with millions of chairs and tables, cabinets and ornaments, candleholders and picture frames and things like that, all of which were sitting targets for the dust that it was our job to get rid of.

It's good to have a lot of stuff to do, though—that's one of the things I learned. It keeps your mind focused, and it makes it a good bit easier to sleep at night. But as busy as we were all morning with our cleaning chores, and all evening helping in the kitchen with dinner—something great happened most afternoons at Blackbrick. And what happened was that a delicious kind of silence would settle on the house and the whole place seemed to swell with strange feelings of freedom and possibility. The three o'clock bell would chime in the hallway and Mrs. Kelly would head off with a steaming teapot to her quarters, and nobody would see her again until she bustled into the kitchen much later to get started on dinner.

It's those afternoons and how they belonged to us that I remember best. The three of us got used to galloping around the hidden corners of Blackbrick. Somerville and Ross got faster and fitter, and they were proud and strong and fun to hang out with.

I can sometimes smell the Blackbrick wind in my face still, and hear Kevin's laugh and see Maggie's very pale cheeks turning red in the cold air. We never cared if it rained, even though Maggie's hair would stick to her face and our noses would go numb, and when we were finished, we'd have to rub down the horses with dry rags, and then run back into the house shivering and dripping and cursing the cold. There were brilliant bright days too, when the sun was a giant splash of gladness, showing off the cold crisp sky, clear and perfect. Maggie and Kevin were brave, and they were young. If you'd seen them the way they used to be, you could never imagine either of them ever being delicate or afraid or old or forgetful or anything like that.

We developed this special way of whispering into the

horses' ears, which made them run really, really fast. And when they did that, we sometimes felt we were going to tumble off their backs, possibly killing ourselves. But we never did fall, and gradually we realized that we never would.

After a while hanging out with Kevin and Maggie became an ordinary, everyday kind of a thing to do.

Maggie loved going down to the south gates to look at the old lodge, and she often asked if we didn't mind going there and having a look together. It was illegal, I kept reminding her, and besides there wasn't much to see. On top of all that, it was tormenting for me to go near the south gates—I didn't like to think about the people on the other side and how I had abandoned them. Plus I wasn't that interested in getting caught down there again by George Corporamore, so most of the time I tried to stay away.

The gate lodge was nothing but a crooked little house, a ruin really, but Maggie always said she liked the idea of doing it up and living in it. She said a small house like that, with a cozy fire and good company, and what else would a person need in life? I said she really should start raising her aspirations a bit more.

We learned to cook dinners, and Mrs. Kelly sighed and said, "Remember, Kevin, the lovely dishes that Bernie Doyle used to make?" Bernie Doyle had been the cook. Apparently nobody could ever have lived up to her legendary status, no matter how hard they tried. Maggie was put on Cordelia duty and had to take her breakfast every day. She didn't even seem to mind that much.

We trained the horses until they could have competed in competitions and won. Whenever we had any free time, we legged it around the corners of the estate that nobody else ever went to anymore on the horses, and shouted various things at each other. We invented an excellent game that involved throwing a potato high up in a big arc and the person on the other horse having to gallop over and catch it in time, and when they did, it was their turn. Might sound kind of stupid, but seriously, it was the best game ever. I'm surprised it's not an actual sport.

Another thing I won't forget is how irritating it is trying to teach people how to read and write. Making up for the past's feeble education system was pretty hard. For one thing, when I was teaching them, Maggie and Kevin kept on chatting to each other and laughing when they should have been concentrating. I started on very easy words, and then a few simple phrases like "The cat sat on the mat." "Guys, concentrate," I'd have to keep saying. "I'm trying to improve your overall levels of literacy. You could at least *look* as if you're making an effort."

Then they might settle down for a bit and get through the exercises I'd given them. It took a long time, but eventually their writing improved and their words got a lot better. I used to get them to write out lines all across the Corporamore notepaper, which was the only paper I had access to, apart from my notebook, which by then was already full.

No matter how much progress we were making, Maggie said we always had to leave Crispin's wing by seven p.m., "in case Lord Corporamore finds you here." Kevin never once asked her what on earth Corporamore would actually be doing there in the evenings, and neither did I, even though it was sort of an obvious question. There were times when I was literally dying to ask her, but I never said another word about it. The night before I'd tried to escape from Black-brick, Maggie had begged me to put certain things right out of my head, and I was trying my best.

Speaking of trying my best, I also did what I could to get Kevin into excellent long-term brain-health habits, but nothing in Blackbrick was a source of omega-3 fatty acids, as far as I could see, except for on Fridays when everyone had to eat mackerel. I wrote out the recipe for smoked salmon pâté in case we ever got our hands on any actual smoked salmon, which frankly was pretty unlikely. But still, when you have knowledge like I had, it's your duty to share it with others who might benefit, so after I'd written it, I pinned it up on the wall in the kitchen. I also wrote a whole load of my own homemade Sudoku puzzles too, which took me ages, and I taught Maggie and Kevin the rules. They caught on pretty fast and got so good that they were soon very bored with them, even when I made them superhard.

They didn't see the point of them. I tried to adopt a positive mental attitude at all times, and I did what I could to get them to do the same.

Everyone says you can't live your life in the past, but I learned to do a fairly decent job of it. It's funny the way time is. Sometimes it feels like it's going to go on forever, and then there are other times when it warps and folds and you don't even know how you got from one season to the next. And besides, even though I'd abandoned the present, it wasn't really my fault. I was a prisoner.

After the day he took the key away, Corporamore didn't ever really say much to me, which was okay as far as I was concerned, because I was never in the mood for having heart-to-hearts with that slimeball. He did come down to the kitchen one day and tell us that someone was to give his daughter riding lessons. Most of the time whenever I saw him coming my way, all I did was try not to look him in the face.

In a Blackbrick winter the place gets so cold that you have to get dressed under the covers of your bed, and when you finally do get out, you have to jump around for centuries before you even begin to get warm.

I never did see another creepy incident with Corporamore and Maggie, which was a relief to me, seeing how basically disturbing that whole particular episode had been. But there were a couple of times when I saw him watching her from a distance, say when she was washing windows or carrying a tray along the corridor to Cordelia's room. And there were other things about Maggie that had started to make me worry.

It began when she got really, really sick. Kevin told me that she was puking every morning. He said it didn't surprise him too much, considering how the food at Blackbrick wasn't what it used to be. After Christmas she stopped feeling sick and started to get fantastically hungry. Hungrier than me and Kevin put together, which was saying a lot.

Christmas wasn't that different from any other time at Blackbrick, at least not for us, except that Mrs. Kelly crept into my room and left two oranges on my bed along with a midget of a chocolate bar. I saw her do it, but I kept on pretending to be asleep. Kevin rushed in to me a few seconds later, saying wasn't it mighty kind of her, and weren't we dead lucky to have gotten presents like that on a Christmas morning, and I was like, yeah, we must have been born under some kind of freakishly lucky star, all right.

Maggie was getting paler and tireder and sadder-looking all the time. She never complained, so it wasn't like anyone was drawing my attention to it, but I am pretty observant and there are things that I notice that other people never seem to see.

In a Blackbrick spring the sunshine is like big solid bars glaring right down onto your face and making you have to squeeze your eyes together quite tightly. And birds start to tweet and twitter outside your window and they sound delighted with themselves.

And in a Blackbrick summer everything grows wild and tall, and the solid sunshine bars gleam inside the rooms so that you can see a million sparkling particles of dust floating around like miniature galaxies. And even when it *is* summer, the basement where I used to sleep never gets warm, and the stone walls stay damp and cold. There was no point in complaining, because complaining got you nowhere in Blackbrick, no matter how reasonable your complaint was, unless you were Cordelia, and nobody wanted to be her.

Over the months Kevin's hair got longer and he got quite a lot more grown-up-looking and a good bit thinner. Which at the time was funny, considering how much fatter he thought Maggie had gotten. He wasn't trying to be rude about it or anything, but it was true.

I guess I knew all along what the situation was, but she didn't talk about it to us and we didn't talk about it to her, and the longer silence grows around something, the easier it becomes for everyone to put it out of their minds. It's called denial, which nobody had ever heard of at Blackbrick, but it's basically the only way to explain how we all ignored Maggie's condition.

And I'd been promoted. Instead of a temporary gofer, by then Mrs. Kelly said I was an assistant stable boy. I was proud of myself, because I'd put in the time and I'd earned it.

Kevin and Maggie didn't just learn to read and write. They became literary know-it-alls, which was a bit irritating, seeing as it was me who'd taught them the basic skills.

I'd say that by then, if they'd been in my class, they would both have passed everyone on the reading scale. When the midafternoon stillness settled on Blackbrick, I'd often find them in the kitchen bent over a book, or sometimes even in the room next to Crispin's, where they'd have lit a fire and where Kevin would be lying on his stomach on one of the old sofas, swinging his legs, and Maggie'd be on the floor, stretched on her back with her hands behind her head. Kevin would read aloud—a whole load of complicated, classic, dead long books. Whenever I saw him doing that with her, it always made me feel a bit jealous.

You don't miss people with the same intensity all the time. You can spend days, weeks even, not thinking about someone, and then all of a sudden something reminds you, and it's as if you've been shot in the face with a sadness gun.

Even though I tried to forget, there were times at Blackbrick when I thought about my mum. When she first left, I didn't think she could get any farther away. Now she might as well have been on another planet. I missed my old granddad, too, even though I wondered how I could, seeing as I was living in the middle of his childhood. I was more or less sure he would be missing me, no matter what everyone was saying about his banjaxed brain.

A few times, when those kinds of things went through my head, I'd pull Corporamore's study apart when nobody else was around, trying to find the key to the south gates. I searched in the kitchen drawers and in the old cupboards and through the lidded boxes that sat on top of the dressers in the pantry. One night I had what I thought was a superbly simple idea—I thought it had been staring me in the face all along, which made me realize that I might not even need the stupid key. I brought a rickety warped ladder from the stables down to the south gates and I climbed over, quite pleased with myself until I realized that there was no future on the other side, only the same old past, and I had to climb back in again feeling like a total idiot.

And then there were other times when I didn't try that hard at all. Eventually I stopped trying altogether, and as I said, things grew normal and routine. Everything becomes ordinary in the end, even living in a different time zone.

People think that the past always stays the same, but that's not true. The past changes exactly the same way as the present does, and people in it change too, and the person who changed most was Maggie McGuire—though, as I said, she never ever complained about anything, which made it easier for us all to keep on pretending that she was okay.

There was one person who did complain and who kept

on complaining and who looked like she would never stop, and that was Cordelia. Over the months, she seemed to discover whole new oceans of demandingness and obnoxiousness, but we had to put up with it, and we weren't supposed to say anything to her.

I wanted to tell her how spoiled and mean she was, but it's funny how some things are difficult to say. Cordelia kept on being able to do what she liked, and we had to keep on accepting it. It was to do with something that Kevin and Maggie called the pecking order. I'm not saying I liked it or anything. I'm just saying that's the way it was.

I think it was nearly summer when Maggie got obsessed with apples. They were the only things she wanted to eat, and she didn't really have an interest in anything else. She said she woke up with images of apples in her head. She said she dreamed of apples, red and crunchy and sweet. She said she might go into a decline if she wasn't able to eat them. If Maggie had had cravings for potatoes or turnips or jam or onions, then we would have been grand. The Blackbrick pantry was full of stuff like that. It was Kevin who suggested that it might be a good idea to have a look in the orchard. "That's normally where you get apples," he said cleverly.

So the two of us went to the orchard, where the trees hung over into the courtyard. Except that there were no apples because apparently it was the wrong time of year. But after a bit of searching around, we found this shed with wooden buckets that were full of apples that somebody must have stored from the season before. We ran back to the kitchen, where there were big stringy, muddy sacks with dirty potatoes in them. We emptied one of them out, making a big potato mountain in the pantry. Back in the orchard shed, I stood at the door keeping watch while Kevin filled that old ropy sack with apples from the wooden buckets. Apples for Maggie.

We carried them to her room, the two of us feeling very proud of ourselves, dragging that massive sack behind us. We told her that we'd risked our lives to get them, which might have been a slight exaggeration, but in fairness, the whole thing had actually been quite difficult.

"Oh, Kevin, Cosmo, you're as kind as anything." But she explained that she suddenly didn't want apples nearly as much as she used to. "It's milk that's the only thing I'm dreaming of now," she said.

"Thanks for keeping us posted," I said, feeling a tiny bit annoyed.

But I kept hearing her voice over and over in my head telling us how we were as kind as anything. And Maggie had this special way of saying "oh" that always made my heart flip over. Sometimes I hear it in my dreams still, but not very often.

Chapter 17

IT WAS hard to stay annoyed with Maggie for too long, no matter how often she changed her mind. Her face was still pale and oval and her hair was still all curly and messy and she was basically still gorgeous. Even more gorgeous, actually. When someone is as lovely as she was, you sort of want to do things for them even if you think occasionally that maybe they're being a bit demanding.

Kevin did say that he was getting kind of tired of being at her "beck and call" the whole time and responding to all her whims. But I didn't mind too much at all. When she asked me if I could possibly do Cordelia's breakfast again once in a while, there was a part of me that was actually happy.

"Do you consider that girl to be your friend?" Cordelia asked me as I was trying to get out of her room one morning, not long after the apple heist.

"Yes, I totally do."

"Well, I'd watch out if I were you. I don't think she's the kind of person you should be friendly with at all. A boy can get a bad reputation very easily, and you wouldn't want to get one, Cosmo, would you?"

I didn't really know what she meant. I said I wasn't all that concerned about reputations. I told her everyone should make up their own minds and not listen to other people's theories. Cordelia replied that in actual fact, reputation was everything, which was the irony of the century, considering how much everybody hated her.

She told me that Maggie was an unchased girl. "Utterly unchased" is what she said. Her father had told her that. I took it to be a very good thing. I told Cordelia that I thought everyone had the right not to be chased, and she looked at me with a big mystified expression in her eyes and a crinkly little frown on her brow.

"Listen, Cordelia, I've got a lot of stuff I need to do, so I'd better go off and do it, right? I'll see you soon."

She spoke to me then. Her teeth were clenched. She said that I was not to take my leave of her until she said so. She said I was an insolent boy, which means "cheeky and disrespectful." She said that *she* was always to be considered the most important chore that I had to attend to. I felt like telling her to flip off with herself.

We ended up having to give Cordelia that riding lesson that Corporamore had said he wanted her to have. She trotted down to the stables in a light-pink velvet coat that swung from side to side, and a stupid hat. Kevin said, "Miss Cordelia, hop up there, and we'll start off nice and carefully." But I whispered the secret fast signal into Somerville's ear, and that brilliant horse ended up clattering off with Cordelia desperately holding on to her neck. By the time we got back, Cordelia's face was light green in color, but she didn't say anything about it, and neither did we.

The next day Mrs. Kelly told us that Miss Cordelia had decided she didn't want riding lessons from us anymore, and me and Kevin gave each other a high five in the cellar.

One afternoon not long after that, Maggie McGuire disappeared. The sun was like a big blob of honey dribbling out of the sky. We had finished all our chores, and we went off to hang out with Maggie like we often used to. When we got to her room, everything was neat and tidy and all her clothes were gone, and there was this little note on the pillow of her carefully made bed.

Part of me was proud. The letters were perfectly formed and only a few of the words were spelled incorrectly, and there was nothing wrong with the grammar at all. But still, even though it was a well-written note, it was one of the worst things that I've ever read on a piece of paper of any kind:

Dear Kevin and Cosmo, I am leveing this house today, and I do not think that I will be back. I wish I could stay here with you both, but I cannot so I'm afrade there you have it. Thank you for your frendship and your kindness. I will never forget it as

long as I live. Please don't try to find me. I must leve
and I beg you not to folow.

I don't know if you've ever looked for someone and they're not there. It's a lousy feeling. Your skin goes all sweaty and you keep going back to places that you've been before, kind of knowing that you're not going to find them but looking, searching, looking all the same, and your heart starts to go really fast, and you can't think about anything else, and you begin to think that you'd do anything at all that you possibly could to find the person you are looking for. I remembered the way my mum had told me she was going to Australia, and how I hadn't said a word, how I'd pretended I didn't even care. I should have told her the truth: I should have said that it was definitely not okay for her to leave me like that, that I needed her to stay with me.

I wasn't going to make that stupid mistake again—not this time, not with Maggie.

I started calling her name and then shouting it, and then eventually I screamed, "MAGGIE, MAGGIE, MAGGIE," over and over again as if I was practically insane.

Eventually Kevin said it was no good. That we'd have to go to bed and start looking for her again in the morning. I said, "Are you seriously telling me that you're going to be able to sleep?" And he said probably not but we'd better try because there was no point in the two of us being totally wrecked on top of everything else.

I pretended to go to bed. But as soon as Kevin said good night and closed his door, I went straight out again.

My hands and my legs were shaking when I swung onto Ross that night, and we galloped, trying to break the sound barrier, feeling as if we were going faster than any human being and horse had ever gone before, so that we could find Maggie.

I wasn't going to give up. I didn't think I ever would. I was sure she needed help. It was only after we'd trampled almost everywhere else on the estate that I thought about the gate lodge. It was one of those moments that you have in life when you ask yourself why you hadn't thought of something sooner.

By the time we got there, Ross and I were dog-tired, but we didn't care that much about ourselves. I tried to open the front door, but it was locked from the inside.

There were a few long, thinnish wooden logs lined up in a sort of pyramid shape alongside the house. I picked one of them up. It was hard to keep my balance, so I staggered around for a bit.

I held the log as steadily as I could and then I ran, roaring, toward the door.

The house was creaky and damp, but someone had tried their best to clean it up. There were broken old chairs propped against the walls, and someone had put wildflowers into a chipped cup that was sitting on a table. I heard a noise in the next room.

It was her. She was there. Which just goes to show, you should listen to your gut instincts every so often.

She was lying on a mattress on the floor. And for a moment I didn't notice anything else except her face, but then there was this little bleating, grumbly sound and I looked among the ragged blankets that she was surrounded by, and that's when I saw the baby, all tiny and squirmy and pink.

"Maggie," I said, moving closer to where she was lying. "Maggie, why didn't you ever *say* anything?"

And then the little baby's eyes looked straight into mine without question or judgment or fear. I kept on looking at the way her mouth moved and how her fingers jerked and her eyes flickered open and closed and her legs stretched out and how little puffs of newborn breath went in and out of her extremely small nose.

I even held her for a little while in my own arms.

Her miniature hands kept opening and closing as if she was trying to cast a spell on the world. Some people say that newborn babies can't see much, but when I held my finger in front of her, she looked straight at it. And when I opened and closed my mouth like a goldfish, she copied me. I swear. Check it out on the Internet. Newborn babies do actually do that. They have this inbuilt ability to copy the people they see around them in quite sophisticated ways almost as soon as they are born. And they're designed to survive.

So even though you might be very worried about how small they look, they have a great instinct for protecting themselves. Apparently if you put their hands against the branch of a tree, they'll cling on really tight and dangle there, hanging on and not falling. I didn't try that, though. To be honest, I wouldn't really recommend trying that with any new babies you happen to know.

The whole time Maggie kept looking at this tiny new person in a totally special, kind, fierce sort of a way. I wanted to do something then. It was an urge I had. Not a dodgy urge or anything. I just wanted to hold Maggie's hand. That's all.

It was a feeling beyond logic or anything that scientists or researchers or theorists can explain in words or in pictures or in diagrams or in anything else. It's that thing that's always there. That thing that's ancient and deep. That thing that never goes away.

Her hair was even messier than usual and strands of it were stuck to her forehead. I brushed them away from her face as I had dreamed of doing, except in my dream the circumstances were completely different.

She asked me how I'd known where to find her. I said I would have kept on looking until I did. She said she had wanted to do this on her own, that she didn't want to drag anyone else into her situation, that it would be much better if nobody knew about it.

And she obviously wasn't in the mood to explain how this had happened, plus I didn't really think it was the right time to ask her. And she kept on asking me what was going to become of her, and she kept wondering aloud how she was going to take care of the baby now that the baby was born, and big tears kept on sliding down her face. I tried to cheer her up by telling her a few jokes, and I'm not a hundred percent sure but I think that was a bit of a help, because she wiped the tears away with the back of her hand. Images of George Corporamore crept around in my head: of him feeling Maggie's shoulder that night in the hall, with his pointed fingers, and of him always looking at her as she passed by. I thought about how I wanted to hurt him and kill him and tell him to stay away from her and not to touch her and to leave her alone.

I'm not somebody who turns my back on my responsibilities. I stick around when people need me. I'm not trying to sound like a saint or anything. It's just that I think that's important. Even if I am only a kid.

The baby started to cry a little bit, but I sang her a song for babies that I knew really well. It's got all these words about the first time you see a baby and how you want to keep them warm and safe and stuff. She stopped crying, which was the whole idea.

I gave her back to Maggie. The three of us fell asleep in that broken-down wreck of a place. Maggie and the baby on the old mattress, and me on the floor beside them. And that night, just for a little while, I stopped worrying about everything. We slept a certain type of sleep that can only be slept by people who have done something very important.

You can't be worried all the time. Sometimes you have to take a break from it.

Chapter 18

IT WAS difficult to believe that someone so pointy and hard and ugly could be the father of someone so soft and round and perfectly beautiful. Apparently as soon as Corporamore had found out that Maggie was going to have his baby, he had told her that she had to leave and had forced her to pretend to everyone else, including me and Kevin, that she'd decided to leave of her own accord for no particular reason. She was too ashamed to go to her parents, and she didn't want to be a worry to them, seeing as they had a load more children to feed already, which is why she ended up in the rubbish gate lodge with the wind whistling through it and no proper toilet or running water.

We didn't get to complain about the behavior of George Corporamore, even though it probably would have done us a world of good. There wasn't time.

I didn't need to talk about what we were going to do next, because I had decided that we were going to smuggle Maggie and the baby back to Blackbrick, at least for a few days while we figured out a plan. Ross, one of the coolest horses of all time, had waited quietly outside the gate lodge for practically the whole night. Now everybody needed to be somewhere that was warm and where there was food nearby.

The baby was small and pretty quiet. It was going to be easy. I told Maggie I was going to take Ross back up to Blackbrick and that I'd be back to get her with Kevin and the cart. She was totally okay with it, but I wasn't going to wait around, just in case she changed her mind.

"By the way, what's her name?" I asked.

"Nora Cosmo McGuire," Maggie said, looking down at the baby as if there was nothing else to worry about. "Nora for short."

I woke Kevin up. "What's happened?" was the first thing he said, because when you have something important to tell someone, it must be written all over your face. I told him how I'd found Maggie, and for a second he was delighted, slipping out of his bed and hopping around on one leg trying to get his trousers on, saying, "Well, that's a relief."

Then I told him about the baby and he fell over.

"A baby? A real baby?" he said when he'd recovered enough to start quizzing me. "What's going on, Cosmo? Why didn't you come and fetch me? What the bloody hell . . . ?"

I thought he deserved to know then, about that time I'd seen Maggie and Corporamore in the shadows. But as soon as I explained, I was sorry I'd even opened my mouth. His jaw tightened and he got a look on his face that I'll never forget. His hands curled up into hard fists and he kept saying something under his breath.

"Cosmo, get out of my way. You've been in my way since you came here. It should have been me. I'm the one she needs. I'm the one who should have been with her all this time. Not you. Not George Corporamore."

I told him that if he came with me and if he just saw Maggie and the baby, he'd probably calm down.

We hitched Somerville and Ross to the cart, which was easy because by then we were professional experts at it. But Kevin didn't look at me or talk to me at all, not like he usually did. And his face was set in a grim clench and it stayed like that until he saw her.

"Are you all right, Maggie?" was all he could say for a while, but he wasn't smiling and his face wasn't soft the way it usually was when he looked at her.

She held Nora out for him to see. He bit his lip, and very quietly he whispered, "How, Maggie? Why?" Maggie closed her eyes really tight and shook her head from side to side and pressed her lips together, and basically it was obvious she was never going to be in the mood to answer questions like that. Then the baby made this little gurgling squeak of a noise, which lightened the atmosphere a bit.

"What do you think of her?" Maggie said eventually, and

Kevin had to admit that she was a smashing-looking child, just like her mother.

We found this massive floppy old sock, and it fitted perfectly on the baby's head. Maggie fed her real breast milk, and me and Kevin weren't even embarrassed. After all, I guess that's one of the reasons for boobs.

We walked out of the gate lodge like a group of injured soldiers. I looked back at the south gates, even though I never really liked looking at them. I thought about the night I'd first arrived, the night that I shook the gates and screamed up into the sky.

It was a bit hard for Maggie to walk. We helped her onto the cart, and then very carefully we passed the baby to her. Maggie winced a few times as we moved the horses as gently as we could up the avenue. I could tell from the way that they were walking that they knew they were pulling something very precious, and baby Nora kept sucking away the whole time. Me and Kevin were tenser and edgier than we had ever been, which I thought must be what proper adults must feel when children are born.

I still don't really know why Maggie was so ashamed of having a baby and why she wanted to hide away from everyone the way she did. As far as I was concerned, she should have been completely proud of herself. I mean, having a new person inside your body and then doing all that extremely hard work to get the new person out, and then feeding the new person with your own body. That's an amazing thing. I'd never realized how amazing it was until I was close up to it.

"I'm a sinner, Cosmo," she said to me. "I've done a terrible, wrong thing, and I'll suffer the rest of my life because of it, and I deserve to suffer."

I kept telling her that there was nothing to be ashamed about. I did have a few opinions about Corporamore and what I'd like to do to him, but I kept all of them to myself because you don't want a new parent to be influenced by negative energy. They're exhausted enough as it is, and they can start crying very easily even if you say nice things to them, like for example if you tell them their baby is lovely and stuff like that.

So anyway, we were on our way back to Blackbrick, me and Maggie and Kevin and the baby and the horses, and Maggie was looking down at Nora, who was asleep. And I could feel all these massive waves of worry sloshing around inside me.

And I was thinking how much I didn't want to be worried anymore. About anything. Even though by then I was used to tracking down disappearing pregnant girls and working out rescue plans for miniature infants. You know, nothing too bloody demanding or anything.

Mrs. Kelly must definitely have known all about Maggie's situation, because when we knocked on the door of her basement quarters and explained what had happened, she said, "Oh, Jesus, Mary, and Joseph, so soon?

"Is everything all right? Are they both quite well?" she asked, and I said they were fine but that it would be really handy if Maggie and the baby could stay with her in her quarters because that way Mrs. Kelly could keep an eye on them.

"Of course they can. Where else would they go, with me rattling around and so much room on my hands?"

Maggie had been waiting outside, holding the baby and swaying slightly to and fro. But we told her to come on in, and as soon as she was inside, she was all, "Oh, thank you, Mrs. Kelly. I'm so very grateful to you. Oh, God bless you." I thought it was a bit over-the-top, to be honest. I wished she'd stop saying that. It's up to people to help babies. Nobody should feel grateful about it. That's just what humans are supposed to do.

And as soon as Mrs. Kelly saw Nora, she was enchanted like everyone is when they see a new person, all sweet and squirmy like that.

Kevin and I cut an old mattress and stuffed it into a bottom drawer in a chest of drawers in this small corner of Mrs. Kelly's rooms. I wasn't at all sure it would satisfy safety regulations for newborn infants, but after a bit of squabbling that got slightly nasty, we calmed down and finally agreed that it was going to have to be good enough. On the floor beside the drawer we made up a bed for Maggie.

I wish I could show them to you, with their black hair and their big round eyes and their serious mouths and their pale faces. I wish I could show you what they were like.

Maggie was pathologically thirsty and kept on asking for more milk. It's quite hard to transport milk down a rickety old staircase in secret when you're in a hurry and when all you have to carry it in is a tin can with a weird curvy handle.

I know it's everyone's duty to take care of babies, but still they have to be lovely to survive. Otherwise, after a while, people would throw them in the corner, because even though they're very small, they are also unbelievably high-maintenance. Their cuteness is their secret weapon. It makes everyone want to do everything for them and keep them clean and more or less behave like their personal slaves.

After the baby was settled in and we had put everything into a manageable holding pattern, I went to the kitchen to give Mrs. Kelly an update. How many times Nora had fed, how Maggie looked, stuff like that.

It was around that time that I began to feel radically left out. Everybody had a focus, and in each of their cases that focus wasn't me. They were getting on with their lives. After all, that's what people have to do, and if I didn't do something to get on with mine, I was going to end up being a third wheel forever.

For the first time in ages, I wanted to go home. It became like a banging in my head. I kept imagining my grandparents searching around, shouting for me, just like I had done for Maggie. I thought maybe that Mum might have decided to come back, and maybe she was looking for me too. And I realized something that's hard to explain—something to do with love, and I felt terrible about the stress that I must have created by disappearing off in a taxi that night and not coming back.

I'd let myself forget about the future and the people in it, but the future was where I belonged. You have to live in your own time zone. You can't live in someone else's. It goes against the natural order of things.

I don't know exactly why, but Brian popped into my head too, as though he were alive for a second with his own face right in front of mine. If Brian hadn't bloody well died, then nothing else bad would ever have happened. My mum wouldn't have become a workaholic and gone off looking for business on the other side of the world. Granddad's brain wouldn't have wanted to erase everything it had once known. Everyone wouldn't have been tormented the whole time thinking about what an idiot Brian was to fall out of a stupid window.

I mean, seriously. Who does that? People are supposed to have basic survival instincts. At least that's what I thought.

If it wasn't for Brian, I wouldn't have ever even met Dr. Sally or any of those losers. Taxi Guy wouldn't have brought me to Blackbrick. I wouldn't have been abandoned in someone else's past.

People tell me that it's bad enough having a brother who's alive. But having a dead one really sucks.

I was tired. I should have gotten used to it. I should have accepted it by now. I should have been over it. And I should have been all right. We all should have. But none of us was all right. My granddad was demented and sitting there like a vegetable. And my mum. Where *was* she, for Chrissake? Sydney? Who goes to Sydney? I mean if you're going to go off and leave everyone when everyone needs you most, surely you could think of somewhere better than that. And Ted? He was too busy being a pioneer of cutting-edge science to worry about me.

These were the things that began to go through my head, but by then I didn't have anyone to talk to about them anymore, because Maggie was obsessed, obviously, with the baby, and Kevin was more focused on Maggie than ever, and Mrs. Kelly was busy shining over all three of them like this big benevolent protective sun.

And I was back on Cordelia duty.

Cordelia said she knew something was up. I asked her what she knew, and she said that she knew Maggie was going to have a baby. I didn't tell her the baby was already here. She started saying how there was something terribly wrong about Maggie still being under the Blackbrick roof, still being sheltered by the generosity of her family when "in truth, by now Maggie should be out on her ear" for being about to have a baby when she wasn't even married.

Something rose inside me then. Something brave. I don't really know why. I guess it was just that there were certain things I wasn't in the mood for anymore.

And the time to be polite and well behaved felt like it had gone. So I put the breakfast tray down on the bed, and I sat down myself, quite close to her.

"Get off my bed this instant!" she whined.

I told her that I had something to say, and then without waiting for her permission, I said it:

"First of all, Cordelia, I never want to hear you talk about Maggie McGuire like that again."

"Oh, really? And what will you do about it?"

I'm not a million percent proud of the way I behaved after she said that, but she was being pretty provocative.

I toppled the tray over, and the bacon smeared greasy stains on her frilly white bed and egg dripped in yellow plops and the teapot crashed to the floor. Cordelia started ringing this stupid little bell and shouting, "Help, help!"

I took the bell away from her and told her to shut up.

"Do you know that there are kids not much older than you all over this country, working every day until their knuckles bleed? Do you know that one Maggie McGuire is worth, like, about five million Cordelia Corporamores?"

Cordelia was quiet for ages then and she looked out

the window, and I explained how even when people acted politely to her, it was only because they felt they had to. It wasn't actually because they wanted to or anything. And I asked her how she thought she would feel if people behaved toward her the way she behaved toward everyone else. I'm not sure how long my lecture went on for. All I know is that once I started, I found it more or less impossible to stop.

She said she was going to have me kicked out of Blackbrick, and I was all like, "Yeah, yeah, yeah, whatever."

And then I asked her why she was always so mean. She said it was none of my business but that if I must know, she'd had a rotten time in her short life. She said that everyone basically ignored her. That she had had a brother who'd died.

So then it struck me that it might be quite lousy to be her, too, which was another big first for me in the realization stakes.

"Cordelia, you need to know something: there comes a time when you've got to stop using your past as a license to do whatever you want. There comes a time when you have to get over things like that and get on with being the best person you can be. If you let the past determine your future, you're probably screwed."

You don't always know how true something is until you say it out loud to someone else.

I was beginning to feel a bit bad about the mess I'd made in her room. I started cleaning up. And then, quite surprisingly, Cordelia got out of her bed and began to help me.

"Am I really so very dreadful?"

The way she said it was kind of trembly and unsure, and her voice sounded little and shocked, the way someone's voice is when they've just realized something about themselves that they'd prefer not to have known.

"Yes, you are. Dreadful. That's pretty much the word, but the good thing is, you see, that now that you know, you have your whole life ahead of you to do something about it."

And that was when Cordelia Corporamore, the spoiledest brat I'd ever met, said something to me that I'd definitely never heard her say before. She said she was sorry. She went even further than that. She said that she didn't know how Kevin and Maggie and me had put up with her for all these months. She said that her horrible behavior was like a prison that she couldn't get out of. I told her she should consider herself lucky, because if she thought about it for a second, it was the kind of prison that she could easily walk away from whenever she wanted.

"Look at me," I said to her. "I'm stuck here. This is a real prison for me. I used to have a key to get out of it, but your father took it off me one night last winter and now I think I'm pretty much here for good, and I want to go home, but I don't think there's anything I can do."

"I am a dreadful person and I'm bitter, and I was jealous of the three of you," she said as if she hadn't been listening.

"Jealous of us?"

"Yes," she said. "You were always having such a tremendous time, and I felt left out. I wanted to spoil your fun. That's what Blackbrick does to people. It makes people hard and cruel, and I think that everyone should try to stay away from here as much as they possibly can."

"Thanks, Cordelia. Thanks for the advice. I have to go now." She looked very small and actually a little bit pretty. "I hope you have a nice life," I said.

"I hope you do too," she said back, and I walked away, closing the door quite gently behind me.

Chapter 19

WHEN YOU'VE decided to leave a place, you get a new energy and it swirls around you like a force field and affects everything. But I didn't know if there was anything I could do to get out. I went down to the south gates and I shook them just as I had done before. A strange, faint smell of something urgent and hopeless lurked in the air. And I really did think that I was always going to be the ghost of the future, stuck in an endless routine in Blackbrick.

But sometimes you get a gift just when you need it most, and the person who brings it is often the person you least expect it to be.

It was right after that despairing session at the gates, and when I was walking back up the south driveway, kicking bits of gravel here and there, that I saw someone running toward me. I hoped it was Maggie, come to tell me all the things she wanted to say, like that she had heard that I was trying to leave and to beg me: "Cosmo, don't go, my life doesn't make sense without you, etc." But as you know, the people who run toward you at Blackbrick are often not the people you want them to be, and this time it was Cordelia.

She was holding something. The thing she was holding was small and silver and bent and dented. She handed it to me. She was out of breath and she put her hands on her knees and panted there for a little while. "Listen," she said, "just listen. This is the key—the one to the south gates that you need." I obviously already knew that. She told me that she had stolen it from her father. If he ever found out, she was going to be in serious trouble.

"You can get out whenever you like now," she said.

I guess I should have felt happy, but I didn't know what I felt anymore. Lots of things. Tired, mainly.

She said I shouldn't waste too much time. There wasn't much point in waiting around, especially now that I had everything I needed. She was sorry about the cruel things she'd thought about Maggie. She said that I should go and visit Maggie to say good-bye because it's important to say good-bye to your friends when you're leaving somewhere. So that's what I did.

"Hi, guys," I said, smiling. I tried my best to be really cheerful, but Maggie must have sensed something in me, because immediately she asked me what was wrong.

"I'm leaving," I said. She stood in front of me with baby Nora squashed up all warm and tight in her arms.

I brushed a couple of little strands of hair away from Maggie's face again then, and I tried to tuck some of it behind her ears, so that I was nearly holding her face with both my hands and looking at her. I touched the bridge of Nora's very small nose. The baby sighed her own shuddery little sigh, but she didn't open her eyes or anything.

Gorgeous. That's what she was. That's what they both were.

I didn't tell them, even though I wanted to. I wanted to say, "Maggie, you are beautiful and you are strong and you are great, and you can do anything you want in your life." There was a funny old camera in Mrs. Kelly's room with a zigzag accordion telescope instead of a zoom lens. I asked Maggie if it was okay if I took a photo of the two of them. Maggie stared straight into the camera all serious, not even trying to smile, with Nora's little velvet head snuggled up close. Taking the camera with me would have been stealing, so I put it back on the shelf, wishing that I could have done something a bit more effective to hang on to the moment. At the last minute I asked her if there was a chance she and Kevin and the baby would come with me.

"Cosmo," she said, "I'd love to. It's just . . ." She looked down at the sleeping Nora, and I guess she didn't need to explain. The thing is that people who've recently had babies have different priorities than boys do. And it really doesn't matter whether they are boys from the past, boys from the present, or boys from the future.

The very last thing I ever said to Maggie was that I'd definitely see her again.

Which is lousy when you think about it.

Because I never did.

Kevin couldn't believe it was Cordelia who'd given me the key. I said I was definitely leaving, and he said he guessed he'd known that this day would come again sooner or later. I asked if he'd go with me to the gates. "Sure, of course I will," he said, and we jogged down the driveway as if it was something we had done together every day for our whole lives. He said he was sorry about how cross he'd been with me about Maggie and the baby. He told me he knew none of it was my fault and that I had been a great help and that I'd never been in the way and that the only reason he'd said I had been was because he was angry. He said he didn't think Maggie was his girl anymore, and I said he should try not to worry about it too much.

He asked me what I was planning to do. We slowed down when we got to the end near the old south gate lodge.

"Who knows what the future holds?" I said, like I was some kind of walking cliché. I told him I was pretty confused, that everything felt completely random and I knew I needed to get out but I wasn't sure where I was going to go. I told him I was lost and there were a lot of things I hadn't a clue about.

I wanted to tell him about everything he meant to me, and I wanted him to put his arm around me and share his cleverness with me and make everything better. But he was still only a kid, and there are times when you want people to do things that they can't actually do.

I told him I had some advice for him, and I asked him to listen very carefully because I was only going to say it once. I said that he should keep exercising and do crosswords and keep reading books and have plenty of friends. Write everything down. And think about his past and all the important moments in his life and good things that he did and the exciting things that happened. And have a positive mental attitude and don't get distressed or anxious if he says something that other people don't understand or believe.

Then I started listing all the dates and times of the lousy things in the world that I could remember. I told him when the planes crashed into the Twin Towers; when bombs killed people in London; when the Asian tsunami made all those people drown, and the Burmese cyclone, and the Chinese earthquake, and the property crash. I tried to remember all the dates and times as accurately as I could. I got the feeling that I was leaving a lot of the world out. But under the circumstances, it was the best I could come up with.

He was full of respect and silence.

I kept the rest as short as I could. I left out a lot of details, because time was running out.

"There's a boy in the future who's going to be your grandson. He falls out of a window on his tenth birthday. His name is Brian. He's not supposed to. It's a terrible accident that happens. And he's only young, and he is supposed to have loads more years ahead of him just like all of us should, and he's great and clever and funny and he has long fingers, and whenever he reads a book, he always hums."

I didn't know if any of this was making any sense to him. It probably wasn't, but I kept going.

"Whatever you do in your life, Kevin, please don't let it happen. It's your job now. You've got to find a way to save him. Remember: Brian is his name. Don't let him fall out the window. It's the only thing I need you to do for me."

He said he wouldn't forget.

He promised.

And I got this feeling that soon there might be no more battles to fight and no more sad things to feel.

"Look, I know that sometimes you'll think about me and doubt that I ever came here. I've doubted it a few times myself. But whenever you start thinking that, I want you to remind yourself that it was true. It is true. It will always be true. And I want you to know how great I think you are, and how sound you have always been and how much I will always remember you. In a million different ways."

I told him that we need to hold on to each other at the times when it matters. It's the way of things. I said that being together, I mean with your family, the people who love you, well, it's very important, and I said how we sometimes have to fight very hard to stay with those people, even if there's a price to pay for it. The price is worth it, I told him, whatever you think at the time.

I thought about my list of crucial people: my mum and

Granddad Kevin and Granny Deedee and Uncle Ted and Brian. And young Kevin and baby Nora. And Maggie.

"Yes," he said, "but sometimes letting go is important too. And we have to learn to do that as well. We have to learn to do it without allowing it to destroy us."

And I think we both kind of knew the hard lessons we'd been trying to teach each other.

"I never got a chance to say this to you before, but you're a total legend," I said. And he said, "A legend? I always thought that a legend is something that didn't happen, something that's not real." And I said, "Well, where I come from, a legend is someone brilliant and fantastic and sound."

"In that case, then, I think you are a total legend too," he said.

"Don't forget me, Kevin," I said to him then. "Please don't forget me."

"Sure, how could I possibly forget? What kind of person would I be if I forgot you?"

"Kevin, please, I need you to promise."

He said he'd do his best.

And I know now that he did do his best. He really did.

I walked over toward the gates, and for some reason I felt this pain deep and dark inside my chest, and I felt hot and cold at the same time and everything was tight and sharp.

I dug into my pocket for the key and I unlocked the padlock.

He said he still couldn't believe how it was Cordelia who had gone to the trouble of stealing the key back from her dad just for me, and I said that maybe she was okay after all and we had probably been a bit hard on her, and I suggested to him that it might be worth giving her a chance.

"Are you really from the future?" he asked, and I told him that yes, I really was, and for the first time it looked like he actually believed me. Something strong and true had crystallized inside me. I think maybe he saw it too.

"This belongs to you," I said then, holding the key out to him.

"What do you want me to do with it?" he asked.

"I'd like you to keep it until you're a very old man, and then one day, in the far distant future, I'd like you to give it to me."

I knew he was going to protect it and I knew how careful with it he was going to be.

And then I watched myself cross over the threshold through those gates as if I wasn't even in my own body.

And I could hear this massive clanking *bang* behind me. It was the gates being shut very loudly. And I tried to look back in through the bars, but everything seemed to disappear and there was all this fog and it was floating around and swirling. Kevin's voice still echoed through the air for a while—saying things about how he was never going to forget.

Chapter 20

I STOOD outside the south gates for quite a while, waiting for something big and possibly fatal to happen. But everything was still. The old noises of Blackbrick trickled away. It was pretty cold, as though all of a sudden it were winter again. And then I realized that I could smell things like rubber and chewing gum and plastic and gasoline—hints and clues like that, wafting through the air. Things I hadn't smelled for what felt like a very long time. I could see bands of blue light in the sky too, a different kind of light from the threads of dawn and dusk that I was used to seeing at Blackbrick.

Everything is different in the present. It doesn't only smell different. It sounds different. There's a constant *buzz* humming away in the background like a machine. And when you open your mouth and taste the air, which you might not think would taste of anything, it actually does have a different flavor. And you can feel something on your skin—the wind of now has a different texture from the wind of then. Even the dark is different. There's a kind of blue light in the present's dark that you don't see in the past. The light of the past is kind of yellowy gold.

It takes a good while for your body to adjust too. When you stand up after traveling back to the present, you immediately fall down again and it takes a few tries before you can walk straight.

I had to crumple up my eyes just to focus on anything at all. And when I did, I could make out the dim light of a car glowing like an alien in the distance. There was a newspaper spread out on the dashboard, and it took me a minute or two to realize what exactly I was looking at.

It was money-pocketing Taxi Guy, with the brilliant people skills.

"Wow," I said, stumbling up to the door and seeing his big elbow leaning on the open window, "You waited. You totally waited for me."

"Yes, well," he said, folding his paper and not looking one tiny bit amazed or surprised to see me, "I did say I would."

The time I'd spent in Blackbrick had been like the closing and opening of an eyelid. It was the exact same time I'd left—the autumn morning of all that time ago, very early.

"Wey hey!" I said, all happy, getting into the taxi. "It's not too late. Nothing's too late."

"Did you find what you were looking for?"

It wasn't any of his business. I told him I hadn't been looking for anything. That I'd just been checking something out. I wasn't even that interested in talking to him, because all I could think about then was that I was going to go home. And I was delighted with myself because I was pretty sure I'd fixed everything. Brian was definitely going to be there, because my granddad Kevin had promised that he wasn't going to let him fall out the window, and I knew he wasn't going to let me down, especially considering how much advance warning he'd gotten. Plus now I had a load of information for Granddad that would help him pass the memory test. Taxi Guy's eyes were looking at me in the rearview mirror, but I didn't care. All I kept saying to myself was, "Sorted, everything's sorted."

I was thinking that maybe I wasn't a loser anymore. I was thinking that maybe I really was a legend.

The taxi man was a pretty sound guy after all. I told him that my brother had been dead for a while, but that I thought I'd reversed the whole thing and everything was going to be okay, and he said, "Buddy, it's a nice thought all right; it would be great if things worked like that, but I don't think they do." And the whole time I kept thinking that he wasn't a Time Lord like me. It wasn't his fault or anything. There were a million things I knew about that nobody else was ever going to understand. I wasn't going to be rude and tell him, so all I did was give him directions to my grandparents' house.

When I got in, I found Granny Deedee lying on the sofa with a scratchy-looking blanket over her. I shook her to wake her up, and slowly she opened her eyes.

"Gran, Gran?"

"Oh, hello, darling. What are you doing back here? Is Ted with you?"

"Gran, I'll explain all that in a minute. I need you to tell me where Brian is."

"Oh dear, Cosmo, do we have to go through all this again?" she said. It definitely wasn't a good sign.

She sat up straight and put out her arms to me as if she wanted to hug me, but I stayed standing with my hands by my sides. I didn't want anyone hugging me, not even Granny Deedee. I only wanted someone to answer my questions.

"Darling, you know that Brian is in everything we do, and he's in the trees and he smiles at us from another place, and that's what's going to have to keep comforting us."

And I said, "Gran. Tell me, will you? Is he still dead?"

I kept asking her that same question over and over again until she answered it. Until she said that yes, yes, of course he was.

"I know it doesn't get any easier, my love. But why are you acting like this? Don't you remember?"

"Of course I remember. Seriously, who does that? I mean, he wasn't a baby or anything. Who falls out of a stupid window? What kind of a moron was he to do something as slow as that?"

My voice was wobbly and I was crying again.

"Hush, Cosmo, there, there. I know. It always seemed so pointless and random to me, too. But we have to learn to live with it. We really do. Otherwise we're all going to lose our minds and our sense of reason, and there's no point in us doing that. It wouldn't be very practical."

There's one thing I can say about my gran: she's always been full of common sense.

But everything felt too late all of a sudden, and something cruel and hard and angry was rising from somewhere very deep and very furious inside me. All I could think of was how I'd gone to this huge amount of trouble. I'd spent practically a whole stupid year in my granddad's childhood, for God's sake, and I'd done a load of things for him. And I'd only asked him to do one thing for me. One measly thing, and he couldn't even do that.

I ran to my granddad's room. He was lying in his bed in exactly the same position I'd left him the very last time I'd talked to him, my poor old granddad, all slumped and heavy-looking. I tried my best. I really did. I tried to see the boy in him. The boy I loved so much. But I couldn't. All I could see was someone who had made a promise to me, with his own voice. A promise that he'd totally broken, as far as I was concerned.

"Granddad Kevin. It's me."

He opened his eyes and gave me the foggy look.

"Who are you?"

"I'm Cosmo, for God's sake, you stupid retard. I'm Cosmo. Cosmo. COSMO. Does that name mean nothing to you? Does this face not ring some tiny bell inside your stupid brain? Don't you know who I am?"

"Oh no. Have I forgotten something?" he asked.

"Yes, as a matter of fact you have. You were supposed to save Brian. You were supposed to stop him from falling out a window."

"Brian? Who's Brian?"

"He was your GRANDSON, you MORON. I told you. I TOLD you. It's the last thing I said when I left Blackbrick. But noooo. Would you BOTHER doing anything about it? He's still dead. Brian's still dead."

Granddad looked at me then. He held his hands up to his mouth like someone who had forgotten something really dreadful and then remembered.

"Don't you remember, you old nutter? You! *You* were the one with the chance to make everything okay. Nobody usually gets a chance like that, but you did, because I gave it to you. And you didn't take it. You wasted it, Kevin. And now everything is wasted and ruined and broken, and it's all your fault."

"I'm so sorry," he said.

"Yes, well, sorry is no good. I guess you'll have to live with that for the rest of your STUPID old LIFE."

I didn't really know why I was talking like that to my lovely granddad. I was already starting to feel like a stupid retard myself. But once you've done something, you can't undo it. The past is frozen.

And then Granny Deedee was standing in the doorway, and she came into the room and she stood between me and him and she started to speak.

"Cosmo? What on earth are you doing? Get away from him. Stop it! How can you turn on him like this when you are the one whom he always adored? He would never have a word said against you, and you two have always been the best of friends. What's gotten into you, Cosmo? Shame on you."

"You don't understand."

"No, I certainly do not. You, young man, are going to have to stop punishing everyone for something that no one can do anything about."

I could tell she was raging with me, not that I blame her or anything.

"I've put up with your selfishness and your tantrums, but this . . . this is simply not acceptable. It doesn't matter how much grief you feel. You're not the only person in the world. I'm losing him too, you know. Day by day he gets further and further away from me as well, into that dark place he's slipping into, and there's nothing I can do. And you come here and you shout at him and you make him so desperately upset when you know we've got to try to make this time as peaceful and calm and gentle as he deserves it to be."

She was totally right, of course. But I couldn't get out of the rage I was in. It seemed to be a bottomless pit there for a while. I started shouting at her then:

"He doesn't remember anything, does he? He's never going to remember anything. All these people he's supposed to love, he's forgotten us, hasn't he? And that's basically that, isn't it?"

I went over to the picture table and held up the photos one by one. And for each photo I shouted a name. Mum! Ted! Brian! Granny Deedee! Me! Me! Me! Me! And I just said "Me" over and over again, which was pretty self-centered, I'll admit. With my arm I swept all the photos off the table, and they clattered and slid and smashed across the floor. And then there was only one picture left. Only one picture that did not fall. It was old and black-and-white and it was of Maggie and baby Nora. Maggie was looking straight ahead, all serious, not even trying to smile, and the baby was snuggled in her arms with her little velvet head peeping out.

I took the photo in my hands and looked down at it. It was still basically unbelievable how good-looking she was. Granddad reached over and he took the photo and he said, "Maggie, oh, Maggie, why did I bring you to Blackbrick? If only you'd stayed away, then you would have been all right."

I could feel the blood all sucking out of my heart and draining away into my feet.

"What? Granddad, what are you talking about? What happened to her?"

But Granddad went back to saying nothing again and there was no point asking him any more questions.

"I'm sorry, everyone," I said under my breath. And I was. I really was.

Granny Deedee was in the kitchen by then, trying to get through to Ted, who never answers his phone. I ran past her, straight out to the shed, and got my old bike, which was quite rusty but it worked okay, and I cycled that morning all the way back to the gates of Blackbrick. I was going back there and I was going to find everyone again, and I was going to make sure nothing bad happened to Maggie.

I cycled really fast. I could see a few faces looking nervously at me from cars and on sidewalks, but I never slowed down and I never stopped. It took a while, but I knew the way. The gates were locked and tied. I lifted a jagged rock from the ground, and I started to whack the padlock as if it were some living thing that I was trying to kill. Again and again I smashed the rock down on the lock with massive force, minding my fingers. Eventually it started to bend and dent and break, and then it fell, with this big, dead *thump*. I opened the gates and I was back. Back in Blackbrick.

I ran up the brown gravelly driveway until I got to the end, but Blackbrick was ruined. Everything was. The windows were broken and boarded up. The big door that had twinkled and glistened at me was gone. There was an empty space where that door used to be. I walked inside, and the hall's old floors were dusty and cracked. I saw the table where the silver tray had always been, but there was nothing there now.

I don't really know why, but I tried to fix a few things.

The handle of the kitchen door was on the floor, with a black steel rod sticking out the back of it. I picked it up and put it back in the hole where it belonged. But it slipped out again and rumbled around, echoing in the empty corridor.

And then I walked up the stairs, all sixty-four of them, even though they were leaning over and creaky and probably quite dangerous.

Blackbrick's skeleton was still there, but its soul had definitely gone. There wasn't any point in hanging around. I did go to the stables, just for a second or two. I'm not stupid; I knew the horses weren't going to be there or anything. I didn't feel anything. Their spirits were gone.

There was nothing left at all.

I ran all the way down the avenue again, past the gate lodge and through the south gates, pulling them closed behind me as tight as I could. By then my legs were very tired and the thought of cycling back to my life felt a bit exhausting. So I lay down and rested my face on the cold ground, and even though it was very uncomfortable, I fell asleep.

Chapter 21

I DON'T really know how long I was there for, but the next thing I could feel was someone's hand on my shoulder.

"Get off me," I said.

"Okay. Sorry, Cosmo," said a voice. "Cosmo, I'm sorry. I'm very sorry about everything and I'm here to ask you if you'll come back with me. We can go back to Gran and Granddad's if you like."

And then I repeated Maggie's and Kevin's and baby Nora's names over and over again, but afterward when I thought about it, I guess he couldn't possibly have known who on earth I was talking about.

It was Uncle Ted. I stood up. Everything felt like it had come to an end and there was something dead somewhere inside me that was making me shiver. He kept on saying how worried he'd been. There was a car waiting, and Ted helped to put my bike in the trunk, and then we went back to my granddad's house.

I sat in the back and kept turning around and looking out the window, knowing that there could never be any more going back, even though I kept wishing that there could.

On the way home Ted said a few things to me, and he didn't sound like the self-obsessed person I'd once thought he was. It was even quite good to see him. I told him it was me who'd stolen his bag, but he was totally fine about it.

I was very tired when we got back, so I fell straight asleep. When I woke up again, I looked around. I was in my own room at Gran and Granddad's. I knew because my lava lamp was throwing its wobbly gentle light around. I was sleeping in my comfortable wide bed and I was covered by my huge white duvet and there were tons of green pillows thrown around the place.

I threw the duvet off. I slid a hand under one of the pillows at the top of the bed and I found my pj's. I wriggled into them and squirmed around there in my old bed for a while like I used to do when I was a kid. The room was all bright and warm and clean. It smelled of lavender.

The next time I woke, I could hear someone singing an old song all about the first time seeing a baby and wanting to hold the baby and keep the baby safe and stuff. I had dreamed of her so often, but whenever I'd opened my eyes before, she'd never been there. This time I wasn't dreaming. Though for a moment, even looking straight at her, I still thought I might have been.

She looked great. She might still have been suffering

from sadness, but if she was, it didn't show that much on the outside anymore.

"Mum . . . Mum . . . Mum . . . Mum . . . Mum." I didn't care how pathetic I sounded saying her name over and over again like that. Like her name was a tune that I knew very well and couldn't stop humming. She wrapped her arms around me and she kept on telling me that everything was all right.

"Mum, how long have you been here?"

She told me she'd just arrived.

"And how did you know? How did you know that this was the day to come back?"

She said she didn't know. She said she'd just been ready to come home to me.

"Why did you leave me in the first place?" I said.

"I'm sorry," she said.

"Why did you have to go so far away?"

She said that when Granddad had started to talk as if Brian were still alive, it had begun to torment her. She said she'd had to get away because she'd been afraid she was going to go crazy. And to think, all this time she'd been telling people it was because the market had dried up.

But anyway she was back now. She'd come back for one reason, and the reason was me. She said she really must have been crazy to leave me, and how she didn't know what she'd been thinking and how she couldn't bear to lose me, too. It was pretty nice to hear her say those things.

I thought of Brian then and all the great things about him and about how much I wished he wasn't dead. I turned over and pressed my face into the pillow. I could hear myself making this strange long small slow sound. She kept her hand on my head.

"I know, sweetheart, I know. I've been missing him so much. I just didn't realize how much you were missing him too. I thought it would be easier somehow if you tried to forget about it."

I told my mum that there's no such thing as forgetting. I told her all the things I remembered about Brian. His long fingers. The dimples in his cheeks that happened when he smiled. The way he used to hum when he was reading books.

And my mum smiled too, and a couple of times we even laughed for a bit. And then we stopped smiling and laughing for another while.

"Granddad was supposed to save him. He was going to do something to save him."

"Cosmo, love. You can't turn back the clock. I've finally accepted that, and now you have to try to accept it too."

But even though I knew that, still I felt like telling my mum that she was wrong. I felt like saying there *is* going back. I felt like explaining to her that I'd *been* back, for God's sake. How I thought I'd gone back for a reason. How I'd thought I was going to be able to do something about what had happened.

⁂ ⁂ ⁂

I've done a lot of research on time travel since then, but even though I've studied it in quite a lot of detail, I still can't really explain what happened to me. There is a physicist in Hungary who reckons that wormholes are bigger than Einstein originally suggested, and that it's not impossible for a whole human to get caught in one, and so maybe that's what happened. And there's this cosmologist in Geneva who's been able to get subatomic particles to travel faster than light, and that means basically that time travel is possible, at least in theory. But I don't know that for sure. I guess I never will.

I'm not a moron. I know that most people don't believe time warps are real or anything. I'm fully aware that mostly they're a trick your mind plays on you when you really want things to have turned out differently than they actually have. I know that. Nobody has to tell me that.

So anyway, I told Mum how I'd shouted at Granddad and been really lousy and mean to him and how Granddad had held his hand up to his mouth and how his chin had trembled and how it was my fault for making him frightened and sad. And my mum said it was all right, everyone understood, and sometimes people do things and they can't help it.

But still for a good while afterward I often played the moment over in my head—that moment when I yelled at my granddad. I spent a good bit of time trying to change it in my head. I have invented this whole new memory, and in it, instead of being horrible, I'm all kind and nice. It doesn't make me feel that much better about it, though. The very second something is done, that's it. There is no taking it back, no matter how much you wish there was.

I tried to explain all this to Mum, and it was a bit confusing and I got all mixed-up and she kept on saying, "Shh, shh," and taking care of me and telling me that it was okay. And for the first time in a very long time, I didn't feel like I had to take care of anyone or rescue anyone or find anyone or hide anyone or feed anyone or comfort anyone. Which was a bit of a relief, to be honest.

After we'd all had a bit more of a rest, I sat at my granddad's old feet and I put my cheek against his knee. He patted my head gently and said, "There, there."

"I love you, Granddad," I said to him, and he said, "I know. I know you do."

"I'm sorry I shouted at you."

"I don't remember you shouting at me," he said.

And then Mum was hovering and talking about having to have lunch out of the way early because Dr. Sally had just called to say she was on her way over. It was kind of sneaky of Dr. Sally. She wasn't supposed to be coming back until the end of the week.

Drat. Granddad and me were sitting there doing nothing when we should have both been studying for the test, and now there was hardly any time.

I took out my notebook, and the two of us made a start.

I told Granddad the whole story of his childhood.

"Do you know what your first job was, Granddad?"

"No," he said, and then I said, "You were a stable boy."

I explained how brilliant he had been with the horses. I said how Somerville and Ross were probably the best cared for horses basically on the planet.

"Do you remember now?"

"Ah yes, a stable boy, of course. That's what I was. The best stable boy in the country."

"Yes, you were. No doubt in my mind about that," I said.

"And we smuggled Maggie into Blackbrick. Do you remember?" Granddad said.

"Well, technically it was me who did most of the work getting her in," I replied.

"Oh yes, it was you. Indeed it was, but I was the one who told you what to say."

He pointed at me with his old brown hands and his half a finger.

"By the way, how did you lose that finger?" I asked him, hoping to hear our joke.

"Isn't it a common accident for a stable boy to have?"

And his old arms mimed the landing of an invisible hammer on his hand. He explained that one little slip into a daydream when you're shoeing your horse, and you'll be lucky to have a single finger left.

"How do you hitch a horse to a cart?" I asked him, and

he reeled off the list of instructions as if he actually were Google.

I asked him how he had learned to read and write, and he said he couldn't quite remember, but that it was something he was always going to have gotten around to, one way or another, despite the obstacles he had faced when he had been young.

We had a pretty good laugh that day. I showed him the drawing of Blackbrick that I'd done at the front of Ted's notebook. He traced his fingers around the shape of it as if he was touching something very precious. He said it was a perfect likeness.

"How many steps from the kitchen to the study?"

"Sixty-four," he said, without even having to think about it.

"Where was Nora born?"

"Nora? Ah, Nora. She was born in the gate lodge."

Granny Deedee came back through the door with tea and biscuits. The steam from the teapot rose in front of her face, and she said, "Are you two still talking about Blackbrick?"

She put the tray down on the table.

"Blackbrick was where your grandfather and I first met," she said then.

I definitely did not know that, I told her, suddenly feeling confused again.

"Blackbrick was my family home."

"Sorry, Gran?" I said. I didn't know what she was saying,

because sometimes you can't see things that are staring you in the face.

"I was born and grew up there. Cordelia Elizabeth Corporamore. I always thought it such a silly name."

My gran was old. She looked old, and her skin was wrinkled, but her eyes were sparkly and you would have known by looking at them that she was smiling even if you weren't able to see the rest of her face. I'd known her my whole life, but that was the moment I first recognized who she was.

Granny Deedee, my own gran. She was Cordelia. God almighty, my granddad had married Cordelia Corporamore. She'd changed her name because of how silly she thought "Cordelia" was. How she came to decide that "Deedee" was a more sensible alternative, I may never know.

She spent a few minutes asking me if I was okay, because she said I'd gone all pale and sort of shocked-looking.

And there in my grandparents' living room I kissed my gran and I hugged her and I said, "Oh, Gran, you turned out lovely. You really did." I'm glad nobody except Granddad saw me doing that, because they would have thought I was definitely a hundred percent pathetic.

It is still pretty hard to believe that I met my own grand-mother when she was young. Okay, the circumstances were freaky enough, but that's what happened. I'd never be able to look at her now without seeing the person she'd once been.

It wasn't the time for dwelling or brooding or debriefing, though, because Dr. Sally was going to be there very soon. Granddad and I spent about forty-five more intensive minutes training his brain and brushing up. We went over some things a few times until I was confident that he was as ready as he'd ever be. Then we got him into a clean shirt and tie, and Granny Deedee parted his hair on the side, kissed him on the cheek, and told him he looked very smart. When Dr. Sally arrived, Granddad welcomed her into the house with the politeness and warmth that you'd normally reserve for a long-lost relative that you'd been dying to see.

He was able to answer every single one of the questions she asked him. Everything we'd studied came up. What his first job had been, how he'd lost his finger, when he'd first met his wife. My granddad told Dr. Sally it was a long story, and Dr. Sally said she had time, and so then he told her all about it. Dr. Sally thought it was a lovely story. I think I even saw her wipe a tear from behind her glasses. He was able to tell us how a carrot was like a potato, even though we hadn't even studied for that one. "They're both root vegetables that grow in the ground. Different colors, though. Different shapes." Dr. Sally said that was an excellent answer and Granddad put his thumbs up and smiled at me, but it was just his gentle way of teasing her. It wasn't as if he had done anything to be particularly thrilled about. The questions were very easy for someone as clever as he was. She nodded her smiley head the whole time like she was dead impressed.

Dr. Sally took ages filling out this form, and then she said, "Mr. Lawless, congratulations. Based on your test results, I'm happy to say that it's still quite appropriate for you to stay here in your own home."

After she left, me and Granddad gave each other a high five, and Gran and Mum came over and all of us did a four-way hug.

"Thank God for that," Granddad said. "I don't care for those tests very much."

Chapter 22

I'M NOT that interested in going into all the details about how my brother Brian died, but basically what happened was that he leaned out of the highest window in our house to wave to me because I was playing in our garden. And he kind of wobbled and then fell, and he made this huge "Whoa" noise all the way down and I thought it was a trick, so I started laughing even though he was dead. When I moved in with my granny Deedee and my granddad Kevin, they said that we wouldn't talk about it anymore and that we'd do our best to put upsetting thoughts right out of our heads, which was fine with me. I hated the way everyone had felt sorry for us, and how they used to talk in these holy voices whenever we were around, the way people do when they're in a hospital or a church. My grandparents didn't want anyone to pity me, because pity is not that helpful. I think they hoped I'd forget the whole thing and get on with my life.

I never did forget. I never will.

I found out much later that Granddad had done his best to save Brian after all. My Granny Deedee said it was the strangest thing, but as soon as Brian was born, my granddad all of a sudden got very concerned about heights. "He was forever going about locking the windows and hiding the keys, and your mother thought he was going mad. He spent all of Brian's childhood warning him about windows and how dangerous it is to dangle out of them. He was assiduous, Cosmo. It got so that he'd hardly let him anywhere NEAR a window. It was as if he already knew what would happen to Brian. And then eventually, when it did happen, well, he blamed himself so very much."

And what happened was that Brian found an open window one day and he loved the wind in his face and being up so high and the way things are when you are looking down on the world, and he leaned out too far, like people sometimes do. He just leaned out too far.

It's lousy, I know, but as soon as Dr. Sally disappeared, my granddad's memory started going seriously south again.

I opened up the Memory Cure website. I hadn't looked at it for a while. Suddenly the instructions looked kind of stupid. I clicked on a link at the bottom that I'd missed, and there was this paragraph that more or less admitted there are some kinds of memory loss that nobody can do that much about. I sort of wish that particular piece of information had been a little closer to the top of the pathetic website.

It shouldn't have been called the Memory Cure at all.

It should have been called: "Try a few useless things to improve someone's memory, and then when they don't work, give up." That would have been a more accurate title.

Later that night I wandered into the kitchen and I looked around. All the Post-its were there, like old soldiers whose jobs are done but who still refuse to leave their positions.

I have all those colored notes. I keep them in a drawer in my own room, and I have a really good lock on it that you can only open if you know this number code, and I'm the only one who knows it. Sometimes, not very often, I take them out and read them. And the one I wrote about Brian makes me feel there is another version of myself out there somewhere, trying to comfort me still.

Just because you can't see someone anymore doesn't mean that they're not part of you. There are people who are gone and dead and there are even people you have never met, and things about them are buried inside you like golden fossils. It could be a saying or an idea or a habit that you have learned from someone in your family who learned it from someone else. It could be the way you pat someone's hand when they need to be comforted. Or it could be the dimples in your cheeks that happen when you smile.

Maggie McGuire died in 1943 of a thing called puerperal fever. It's something that people used to get after they had a baby in unhygienic circumstances or if they couldn't get fairly speedy access to antibiotics. Granddad never talked about it. After Maggie had died, he had wanted to take care of baby Nora, but nobody would let a young kid bring up a baby in those days. Actually, when I think about it, they probably wouldn't even allow that now. In those days unclaimed babies were often sent to horrible places that pretended to be laundries. And babies who went there were treated like prisoners. Kevin had been pretty sure this might be what would happen to Nora, so he begged Mrs. Kelly to keep her safe and take care of her. By then Mrs. Kelly completely loved the baby and was pretty sick of working at Blackbrick herself, so she packed her bags, and even though she didn't have that much money at all, still she was able somehow to take herself and the baby to Boston, which at the time people reckoned was as far away as, say, Sydney is now.

And years later my granddad married Cordelia, who is my gran, and now there's my mum and my uncle Ted, who is actually one of the soundest guys I know, and there's me, and well, you know, the rest is history. Everything becomes history in the end.

Nothing turned out the way my granddad planned it, even though he was brave and clever when he was young, and his plans were usually quite well thought-out in advance.

I googled "Nora McGuire" and found out that she had had loads of grandchildren. I e-mailed one of them, pretending I was doing a project on the history of Blackbrick Abbey for school. And now Nora's granddaughter is a friend of mine on Facebook. She told me that Nora had been brought up in America by her legal guardian, a woman called Mary Kelly. And the reason they'd been able to travel to America, so the story goes, was that someone called George Corporamore had given them enough money to travel there and start a new life. Apparently Nora had always been a wonderful, kind, generous, and very courteous woman, much loved by everyone who knew her, which made me feel delighted and proud, not that any of it came as much of a surprise.

Nora's granddaughter thought it was slightly weird that my name was Cosmo, seeing as it had been her grandmother's inexplicable middle name too. I was about to start explaining it to her when I realized how ridiculous it was all going to sound, so I stopped. "Yeah, it's a freaky coincidence okay," was all I said about it in the end.

There are different kinds of stories about what Lord George Corporamore was actually like. Some said he was lousy and vain and snobbish and condescending and exploitative. Others said that he was a good-hearted defender of the common people and fantastically decent. Hardly anybody knows the truth.

Me and Nora's granddaughter ended up Skyping each other a good few times. I asked her loads more questions. She said I was very thorough and that I was definitely going to ace my project.

Granny Deedee said that the stories of those horses

flying around Blackbrick were like a legend that had survived, but now there aren't that many people around who remember if the legend was true. She remembers meeting Kevin when he was a stable boy and how handsome he was. "Were there any other handsome boys?" I asked her, and she said that before the war there had been lots and lots but their names and faces had floated away in the fog of time, and in any case she only had eyes for Kevin.

She did say how she remembers that everyone had been amazed about how fit and fast and shiny those two remaining Blackbrick horses always seemed to be.

It was all true. It totally did happen. The brilliant horses really were there, and Maggie McGuire was there too, and Nora was born and Maggie was a hero who would have done anything at all to protect her new baby. Maggie would have been fine if it hadn't been for the fever. That and the lack of antibiotics.

And sometimes I can still see Mrs. Kelly standing by the stove in the kitchen at Blackbrick Abbey, and in my mind she's strong and kind and practical and on my side, just like she always used to be.

Chapter 23

AFTER THE whole Blackbrick experience, I took a bit of a break from everything, but my mum said that sooner or later I was going to have to start getting back to normal. I replied that there was no such thing as normal, and I tried to tell her that I was quite resourceful now and could probably figure out a way of taking care of my own education. She was having none of it, though. So I had to go back to school and act as if nothing had ever happened, which was a pain at first.

As soon as I walked in the door, Mrs. Cribben was all, "Class, say hello to Cosmo. It *is* good to see you. Isn't it, everyone?" Patronizing stuff like that.

The very second she turned her back, D. J. Burke said, "Hey look, everyone, Loser Boy returns." At lunch break I walked over to him in the yard. He stared straight at me, snapping his bubble gum the way he always used to. I stared straight back. And then I pulled him to the ground and I put my foot on his chest and pointed my toe toward his chin. I told him that my will was greater than his. I wasn't rude or anything, but I said that I'd prefer if in future he didn't call me that name, or any other names for that matter. I told him I wasn't a Loser Boy. I told him that he didn't have to believe me or anything but that as a matter of fact, I was a legend. He tried to hit me, but by then my reflexes were pretty good and I got there first.

He had to go to the nurse for a while, not that there was anything wrong with him. He made a massive deal out of it. Nobody called me Loser Boy anymore after that.

Very early one morning I went into Granny Deedee's room to see if she was awake, and we got chatting. I asked her to tell me about her brother, Crispin. She said the reason she had never talked to me about him before was because I had enough sad stories of my own, but I said I was ready for it now. So she told me that he'd rescued a load of young soldiers who'd been lying in mud, dying because they'd been shot by their enemies, who were only boys as well. Crispin had been tormented when he had come home, haunted by those memories of war, and the night before he was supposed to go back after his break from it, he killed himself at the south gates. That's why everyone hated people hanging around there. The gates had been locked up the day he died, and nobody was allowed to go through them after that.

She said that she hadn't cared to talk about it over the years, but I could tell it did her good, exhausting as it was to be reminded of such very sad things. I told her to stay in bed and I'd go down and bring her up some breakfast, and she said that would be very nice.

I sliced up a cottage loaf and I did the slices of bacon very carefully and I scrambled the eggs with exactly the right amount of butter. And when she saw me coming back in with the tray, she had this questiony look on her face, and when I put the tray down on her covers, she took me by the hands and she said, "Oh my goodness."

She said it was perfect. All she asked for was an extra spoon of sugar in her tea, because she was feeling a little dizzy.

She looked at me for a much longer time than people normally do, with her big unblinky eyes, and she said, "Cosmo? Cosmo?" and I said, "Yes." And she said, "It really is you." And I was all like, yes, of course it's me. It's been me the whole time. And I smiled at her, hoping the whole scenario wasn't freaking her out too much. "Oh, deary me," she said. "Why did I never see it before?" and I said that some things are mysterious and some things are difficult to explain.

"Thank you for everything, Cosmo. Thank you for this lovely breakfast and for all the other lovely breakfasts. I want you to know that you're a very special boy."

"Special" didn't even get close to describing me. I'm not just special. I'm a Time Legend, that's what I am.

Mum and Ted brought John back from the farm. When I went down to the stables near Granddad's house, John was waiting for me. Someone had taken good care of him after all. His hooves were in pretty good shape. As soon as he saw me, he whinnied and danced. He practically smiled at me.

Me and John galloped again, the way we always used to. In through the trees and the fields and around the hidden corners. We leaped over barrels and old flower beds. We screeched to a halt every so often, and then we were off again. I could hear his breathing, fast and certain. I told him all about Blackbrick and Maggie and Nora and my young granddad, and it didn't matter if he didn't understand the whole thing fully. I could hear his hooves landing with cloppy, thuddy echoes as they grasped for a second on to the ground beneath before rising again. And I could hear someone laughing. For a second I didn't know that it was me. I was laughing the way normal people do. The way I've heard other people laugh when they're going really fast or when they're surprising themselves by doing something they're already very good at.

I sat with my granddad every single day before he died as that last autumn hardened into winter. I always tried to make sure he was as comfortable as possible. I usually held his hand, or at least I patted it a few times to let him know I was there. And even though everyone thought his brain was banjaxed by then, it actually wasn't. It was there the whole time; it's just that other people didn't know. My mum and Uncle Ted told me I should really try to stop hoping for any sign of recognition and not to be sad if he didn't know me. They said that it was going to get harder and harder for me to see Granddad the way he was, considering what a bright, brilliant guy I had always known him to be, and considering how he used to be so clever and sharp and intelligent, known for living on his wits.

But nobody knew what used to happen when it was only him and me and we were able to talk about the past.

There had always been millions of photographs in Granny and Granddad's house, and during those last days I gave him a load more—of Blackbrick Abbey and of the stables and the horses and the driveway and Nora and Maggie. I had to make a few calls to get some of the others, and I had to spend a few hours on the Internet and go on a couple of journeys to get them. But I definitely think it was worth it. Nora's granddaughter sent me a couple of JPEGs of Nora when she was a grown-up. She was totally recognizable.

Me and my granddad had exactly the same conversation a good few times.

"Granddad," I would say. And at first he wouldn't say anything at all. But then I would lean closer to him, and very quietly I would say, "Kevin, it's me. Don't you remember?" and when I said that, he would open his eyes and a massive smile would creep across his lovely old face.

"Ah, Cosmo. I've been waiting for you. I knew you'd come. I didn't want to go without seeing you," he would say, and I would say, "Thanks."

"What happened to the baby?" he would ask.

I told him the baby had grown up, and she had been fine and she had had children and grandchildren. I held up her photos close to his face so that he could see for himself.

I reminded him I'd been there when she was born, and I told him that with my own eyes I had seen her take her first gulps of air as a brand-new person, and I saw her name, Nora Cosmo, settle on her when she was a tiny, squirming, fresh newborn baby, full of a thousand possible futures. And he'd always say, "Yes, of course. I remember now. Trust you, Cosmo. Trust you for keeping me on the straight and narrow." And when he said that, he would look as clear and bright and glittery-eyed as he had ever been.

"I thought it was going to be you and Maggie," I would say to him.

"So did I," he'd say, "but things don't always turn out the way you plan them."

Too bloody right, I'd think to myself.

I told Granddad that I still thought that Maggie dying was the biggest disaster of all, and how I still wished there had been a way that we could have done something about it, and he said yes, it was terrible, but you can repair life. Even in the middle of a tragedy, there's still the possibility of joy. Joy always bubbles under the surface, waiting to break through. He admitted it was difficult to believe when you were in the middle of the tragedy, but he said that I should still always try as hard as I could to remember the joy. I told him I'd do my best.

It was during one of those conversations that I realized who my great-grandfather was. I can remember exactly the moment it hit me, because at the time I was looking down at my fingers. You're so used to your own fingers because they're attached to you that you don't usually think there's anything particularly remarkable about them. But if I look at mine even now, I still notice that they are a bit pointy.

And I thought about the number of times I had wished George Corporamore was dead, and how now he is. Long dead, as my granddad used to say. Maybe even lousy people aren't all bad. He did give money to Mrs. Kelly, and that's what saved Nora from going to a laundry orphanage, so I guess lousiness has its limits.

In any case, I try not to think about it too much anymore. Being related to someone like George Corporamore is the kind of thing that can drive you mad.

"You haven't forgotten me, have you, Granddad?"

Although he was very near the end of his life, still he managed to put this exaggerated pretend crushed look on his face.

"Cosmo," he said, "how can you even suggest such a thing? How could I forget?" and he pointed at me then with his non-existent finger. "For goodness' sake," he rasped, chuckling now, "what kind of a person would I be if I forgot you?"

Then I rested my head on his chest for a while, and he whispered, "You're all right, Cosmo, aren't you?"

I told him that I really was all right.

I told him I was grand.

EPILOGUE

I'D REALLY LIKE it if, after all this, I was able to tell you that when someone dies, you get over it, but I can't say that, and I don't think I'll ever be able to say it. I might still be a kid and everything, but I've grown up a good bit recently. I've stopped begging the world to give me back the things that I have lost. They are gone. I've got to get used to it. But even though they've gone, they've left a mark, and their marks comfort me quite a lot. It's obviously not as good as them actually being here.

I miss Brian and Granddad Kevin an awful lot. There are times when it seems as if there's this massive black brick, cold and heavy, wedged inside my body, impossible to remove. Maybe that's not exactly how other people feel it. But everyone knows what it's like to miss someone. I don't have to explain that. That's what being human is. We're supposed to miss people.

And I've been working pretty hard to try to stop wishing for things that I can't have. I've more or less completely stopped hoping that people will come back to life again when everyone knows they are dead. Hoping for something like that is a huge waste of time. But I do think it's probably okay, once in a while, to have moments when your whole body still aches for someone. Even when you know that they're not coming back.

The ghosts in your life don't ever really go away. Every so often they will whisper to you and they will brush past you, and maybe you will even feel their misty sweet breath on your skin. It's fine. Don't worry about it too much. It doesn't mean they're taking over your whole entire life. Take me, for example. Most of the time I feel more or less grand. But sometimes I can hear things, like Maggie's voice, as clear as it ever was. And there are still times when I would really like, just once more, to feel my fingers touching her face.

ACKNOWLEDGMENTS

Affectionate and heartfelt thanks to Ben Moore for his expert advice, his faith in Cosmo, and for knowing what to do with the key; to David and Paul Moore for always being so interested; and to Elizabeth Moore for more than I can ever say. Also massive thanks to Melanie Sheridan, Sarah MacCurtain, Aelish Nagle, Maura Murphy, Terry Barrett, Fionnuala Price, Fiona Geoghegan, James Martyn, Bob Whelan, Adele Whelan, Eoin Devereux, Liz Devereux, and the entire O'Dea clan. Thanks to my godchildren Stella Byng, Myles Egan, Ashlee DaCosta, and Ella Nethercott, and their siblings, Declan, Mika, Sophie, and Alannah. Also thanks to Ann Fitzgerald, John Consodine, Hugh Fitzgerald, and to Abby and Moya. I am lucky and grateful to have a literary agent like Jo Unwin and editors like Fiona Kennedy and Ruta Rimas—working with them has been a pure pleasure. Thanks to everyone at Conville and Walsh, at Orion Children's books, and at Annaghmakerrig. Love and gratitude to my fabulous Eoghan, my wonderful Stephanie, and my magical Gabriela. Finally, thank you, Ger Fitzgerald, for making all my best dreams come true, including this one.

AUTHOR'S NOTE

My father was a delightful man. Throughout my entire childhood I never remember him raising his voice, except in jest, and he was rarely ever cross. Despite being busy and hardworking, he spent lots of time with me, something that I took for granted. There were, I am sure, plenty of times when most people would have found me exasperating, but my dad always made me feel as if I was lovely and clever and beautiful.

He encouraged me to listen, to read, to think, to travel, to write, and mainly just to revel in the amazing gift that it is to be alive. He was funny and whimsical, very creative and literary, but also very modest—full of a kind of calm, humorous zest. I've never met anyone else like him.

He was diagnosed with Alzheimer's some years ago, a disease that slowly but relentlessly takes someone's memory and identity away. It's hard to describe the bleakness that I felt when I realized that gradually he was forgetting us all. Losing someone to Alzheimer's is a very common experience, but one that remains poorly understood and difficult to talk about.

Memory loss is an important part of the story in *Back to*

Blackbrick. For me, the magic of writing is that even if you start out being dominated by your own experiences and feelings, you end up being able to occupy other people's heads and hearts, and through this, to discover more about the world than might otherwise have been possible. Cosmo, his granddad, and the other people in *Back to Blackbrick* are completely fictional characters with minds and personalities of their own, but together they have helped me to remember that no one who has loved you ever really goes away, and that adventure and discovery wait for us in unexpected places, perhaps especially during sad or difficult times in life.

Sarah Moore Fitzgerald
Limerick, Ireland
March 2012